HORSE SENSE

AND

BIRDHOUSES

By: Amos Moses Terry

ISBN: 1-4107-5382-4 (e-book)
ISBN: 1-4107-5381-6 (Paperback)
ISBN: 1-4107-5380-8 (Hardcover)

Library of Congress Control Number: 2003097673

This book is printed on acid free paper.

Printed in the United States of America
Bloomington, IN

1stBooks – rev. 12/01/03

DEDICATION

As you walk through life, you meet a few (only a few) unforgettable characters. To me, my brother, "Dub" was one of those characters. He was my brother but he was some more of a man. He is dead now but he will always live in my heart and memories.

His name is mentioned often in my book for he played such an important part in my life.

"Dub", as you look down from heaven, I dedicate this book in memory of you, Ole Brother!

Table of Content

DEDICATION...iii
TABLE OF CONTENT..v
ACKNOWLEDGEMENTS..ix
INTRODUCTION xi

CHAPTER 1 : HORSE SENSE.. 1

CHAPTER 2 : NAMES... 13

CHAPTER 3 : BIRDHOUSES AND BIRDFEEDERS............... 19

    DUTCH TWEET... 20
    ONE-EYED JOE.. 23
    BARN OWL BOARDING HOUSE 26
    EGRET'S HANGOUT 29
    WOOD WARBLER'S CABIN... 31
    PAPA'S POUT HOUSE 34
    SEE ROCK CITY 37
    A HOME IN THE STICKS.. 40
    TIN LIZZY 43
    DOBBIN'S BRIDGE... 45
    PROSPECTOR'S CABIN 48
    WHIP-POOR-WILL TOWN HOUSE 51
    EGGING IT ON 54
    OVER THE MOON 57
    TWO LOVE BIRDS 60
    COW BARN.. 63
    BIG DIFFERENCE 66
    OBEY 69
    TWEETY... 72
    THE FEEDING TROUGH 75
    SIDEWALK CAFE.. 78
    THE MEETING PLACE.. 80
    A BIRD IN THE HAND, ETC, ETC 83
    COTTON HOUSE 86
    FRENCH BIRD CHALET... 89
    WREN HI.. 92

"OUR GANG" 95
FIELD LARK 98
"UFO" 100
COUNTRY SHACK 103
BACK YARD FEEDER.. 106
MARTIN FAMILY HOUSING 109
MISS BOSSEY 111
"WHOA NELLIE" 113
"OINK".. 116
BROWN THRASHER'S CABIN 119
WOOD PEWEE 122
THIS PHONE IS FOR THE BIRDS 125
CAT BIRD INN... 128
EL SENORITA 131
THE CROW'S NEST 134
OLD TAR'S LIGHTHOUSE.. 137
LITTLE RED SCHOOLHOUSE 140
MARTIN'S VILLA 143
YODELER'S CABIN 146
RED BIRD CAFE 149
COUNTY JAIL 151
COW BIRDS... 154
OLD NAGS HOME 157
HUNGRY PELICAN 160
ENGLISH PUB 163
"DAT COON" 166
OH! POSSUM 169
FIDO... 172
NIGHT OWLS 175
SNOW BIRDS.. 178
EARLY BIRD CAFE 181
BIG BIRD... 184
BED N' BREAKFAST 187
SLY "BRER" FOX 190
HOUND DOGS... 194
BLUE BIRD CHALET 196
RED ROBIN'S CHAPEL 199
"JERKS" 202
CORNER STATION 204

"WHAT'S UP DOC" 207
DIXIE GAS 210
TEXACO SERVICE 213
BILLIE 217
OZMINT OIL COMPANY 220
FLYING SQUIRREL 223
PETTY COAT JUNCTION 226
ROBIN'S LODGE 230

CHAPTER 4 : BIRD FACTS 233

OLD CROWS... 233
TOUCAN 234
HUMMING BIRD 235
CEDAR WAX WING 236
PARROT 237
BARN OWL.. 238
FROG MOUTHS 239
BARN SWALLOW 240
CAROLINA WREN.. 241
RHINOCEROS HORNBILL 242
PENGUIN 243
ROAD RUNNER 244
TRUMPETER 245
WOOD PECKER 246
SWAN 247
BANTAM ROOSTER 248
CHANNEL-BILLED CUCKOO 249
BALD EAGLE 250
EMU 251
(CAN'T FLY, CAN'T SING) 251
SNIPE... 252
PURPLE MARTIN 253
GULL (YAK! YAK!)...................................... 254
BAT 255

ACKNOWLEDGEMENTS

If you have ever written a book (this is my second – the first was technical) you will realize that you can't begin to list all the contributing sources.

A person's brain is like a computer – it stores information on a hard drive, and, when you press the right button, you can retrieve the information you are seeking. (The older one gets the harder it is to find the right button; however, I think I have pushed the right buttons regarding special characters mentioned in the book).

I used my personal computer when I wrote the book. Seriously, most of the material contained in the book came from ideas, thoughts, memories, and experiences that had been stored in my computer (the cells of my old brain).

I did refer, however, to a few books to glean certain information about birds and their habitats. These books were: Encyclopedia of Birds by Dr. David Kurshner; The American Field Guide to North American Birds, Eastern Region by Bull & Farrand,Jr; and World Book Encyclopedia. In addition, a few characters for names and illustrations of my birdhouses were obtained from comic strips and cartoons found in various newspapers and magazines.

I am grateful for my son, Phillip Terry, an English Major, for editing the book for grammatical exactness. (If you find any mistakes, He "dun 'em").

I am also thankful and grateful for my wife, Imogene, who spent hours typing and retyping. I started typing with my one finger, hunt and peck method, but gave up after my computer failed to save my files – see, that's what I'm talking about in being able to push the right button. Anyway, Imogene rescued me and volunteered to type the book. (She's a real doll and a Southern belle. I wish you could meet her.)

The artwork for the book cover was done by my daughter-in-law, Peggy Terry (my son, Walter's wife). Don't you think the cover is an "attention grabber"? Peggy has a God given talent and she has two daughters and son (my grandchildren) who are also gifted in art. Thanks Peggy!

INTRODUCTION

Several years ago, my daughter, Angie, asked me to write my autobiography. I don't know why she asked me to do a thing like that. She knows all about half of my life. She lived in my house, and put her feet under my table for that length of time. As for the other half, she could have asked anyone around the little town of Iva, South Carolina and they would have been glad to fill her in. (They probably know things about me that I don't even know myself-- people are nosey like that).

What is a biography anyway? Is it facts or is it fiction?

I understand that the biography of former President Ronald Reagan was written by a fellow who was supposed to know the President intimately; but the biography he wrote contained mostly fiction.

This book is neither facts nor fiction. It's a mixture of philosophy, autobiography, fiction and a little bit of facts about birds and birdhouses.

When you browse through the book, I'm sure you will learn quickly that the author is a Southerner--not just any Southerner, but a "True Blue", "Dedicated", Tried in the Furnace" (or should I say :"Tried by the Blazing Sun") Southerner; but my neck is not red.

I have been out of the sun for a while, and I have traveled around the world a few times, and I have learned some things. My old weather beaten heart has softened and I am no longer biased. I believe that all men are created equal.

But.......! I still believe, even after all my travels, that the South is still the best place in the whole wide world. So then, why are some people "hell bent" on trying to change us? (Could it be that they are jealous)?

Come, let's you and me reason together. I ask you: "Is it alright for people of New England to sing: I'm a Yankee Doodle Dandy?" Is that alright with you? Well then, why is it not alright for me and other Southerners to sing "Dixie"? (Some of us worked in cotton fields down South, too, and we had a "Mammy" that loved us!). And another thing: shouldn't people from Virginia be able to sing: "Carry me back to Old Virginny" without being chastised?

Dixie and Old Virginia are songs about the South that I love – not me only, but scores of other compassionate, considerate Southern people. If you are a black, white, red, brown, tan or yellow, Christian Southerner, I'm sure you will agree with me and you would not be ashamed to join with me and help me sing those songs. Did I hear you say: "Amen"?

Don't you agree that the ones who wrote those songs wrote them from a heart of love? They loved their home! They loved the South!

People who want us to stop singing those songs are acting from hearts of malice and vengeance, and hate. These people need to repent and have their hearts cleansed and be made whiter than snow. Then they could join the fellowship of genuine Christian Southerners and help us sing and experience joy, peace, and love like they have never known before.

People who oppose such singing are hurting their own cause. Amos and Andy was one of the best humorous shows of all time. Yet the Bigots had the show taken off the air -- thus hurting their own cause. People should be able to laugh at themselves. People should be able to use their God-given talents to the fullest. If you squash things you do best, you are hurting yourself!

If people want to sing the Blues, Soul, Rap, Country, or Rock (as long as it is clean and no cussing) shouldn't they have that right? You wouldn't call people prejudiced for wanting to have that right, would you?

I know the South is not perfect. It is no Eden by any means; but it is still the best place on the face of the earth where people still love their neighbors! In most other areas of our great country, neighbors don't even know their neighbors' names.

I'm not hiding my head in the sand. I know we do have problems in the South--problems originated long, long ago. We have made some very dumb mistakes. (Lord, I wish we could go back and undo those mistakes).

The mistakes began a long time ago and have been handed down through generations and have become ingrained into the Southern way of life; consequently, the mistakes will not be corrected overnight. It will take a few years.

However, let me assure you that we, the people of the South, understand our problems and we are diligently working on solutions.

If people from other areas, who think they know better than we do, will quit trying to impose their will on us, we will solve the South's problems better and more swiftly. So, if you are from another area of the country, please stay where you are and help your own area solve problems. You have problems, too.

I'll tell you what: "We, the people of the South will let you work on your problems, without us interfering, if you will let us work on ours". Is it a deal? OK then, let's shake on it!

I'm sure the South is big enough, smart enough, and compassionate enough to solve her problems. Let me assure: We will solve our problems and we won't have to surrender every ounce of our heritage to do it! AND LISTEN: "One day we will become the Eden Garden of Brotherly Love!"

I guess you know, by now, that this book is written Southern Style.

A fellow by the name of Phil Harris used to sing, "That's what I Like About The South!"

What I like about the South is so much that I can't begin to express it all in a single book -- it would take volumes and I don't have that much time; but one <u>big</u> thing that means so much to me is the light-hearted humor that you find in the South that doesn't seem to exist anywhere else. The reason for this is that the South is a land where the people are easy-going, simple, and able to laugh at themselves.

I think that most folks take life too seriously. God made this world for us to enjoy. We can't enjoy it if we go around with frowns on our faces most of the time, and worry about what somebody else is doing.

Humor is good for the heart. Life is full of humor if we just look around. Some of my happiest moments were simple things that I thought were funny. I have included some of these humorous events in this book. I hope you will find them funny too.

Life is short. We should live and enjoy every minute of it.

Dried prunes are OK, and may even be good for you; but <u>NOBODY</u> enjoys a dried prune face. So, laugh and you will find the world will laugh with you.

Read my book. Roll it over in your mind. Digest it. Maybe you will enjoy it. I hope it will give you a chuckle now and then. If you find something in it that reminds you of bygone days, tell someone about it (maybe that will give you joy and will also help sell my book).

Have a nice day.

Amos Moses Terry

Chapter 1

HORSE SENSE

The South was different when I was a boy than it is today. Back then; the South was predominately agricultural (cotton was the main crop). But cotton has almost disappeared and in its place one will find highways, subdivisions, shopping centers, and a lot of concrete.

Horses and mules are gone. The South is booming. It's busting its breeches at the seams. To get anywhere today, it is imperative that one have a good education. That was not the case in the old days. At least that's what most parents thought. Horse sense was good enough. Workhorses knew how to plow and that's about all anyone needed to know. College educated folks were scarce because they couldn't find a job anyway except at farming.

I remember one college-educated dude that people laughed at. He wore a coat and tie and a Sunday hat while plowing his mule. People thought that was funny. I guess it was funny for folks who wore overalls and straw hats all the time.

Horse sense might have been good enough back then, and that's about all that most folks had (that explains why they lived in such pitiful conditions), but horse sense is not enough today.

There is an old saying that you can lead a horse to water but you can't make him drink. I say, also, that you could send a horse to college but you can't make him learn. (I saw a horse one time that could count to five by pawing the ground and the crowd thought that was amazing). But I'm sure you couldn't teach a horse to do algebra, trigonometry, calculus, etc. It's hard for some people with lots of brains, like me, to learn that stuff.

1

I don't agree with the old timers (older than me). I think education is very important. My high school algebra teacher thought it was important too. He said one time to the class: "You boys don't seem to think education is important. You say that you are going to be a farmer and that you don't need to know algebra and English and stuff. Well, where are you going to get your mule?" That was a good question. I bet a lot of the boys had not even thought of that.

Another teacher of mine, my agriculture teacher, said to us boys: "I like to smell the aroma of fresh horse manure on a frosty morn".

Yes, I think education is important, but if you try to educate a horse you might get a jackass. Reckon there's any truth to that?

Don't get me wrong, I don't have a thing against horses, but I don't think they have as much sense as people give them credit for having I think pigs are smarter.

I raised some pigs once and they got out of their pen. They roamed all over the countryside. They roamed all over my garden, too, rooting up cabbages, tomatoes, and squash. (I didn't mind losing the squash. I was going to feed most of the squash to the pigs anyway), but they rooted up good things that I liked. I tried to drive them back into their pen, but they would not go back. I chased after them, and they would run and stop and look at me to see what I was going to do next. I would spread out my arms and suddenly they would dart around me, and give a loud grunt, and off they would go. After they did that several times, I decided the pigs were out smarting me. While they were stopped and looking at me, they were resting. I said, ok, if that's the way you want to play, I'm not going to let you rest. I quit trying to drive them into the pen. I just started chasing them. Wherever they went, I was right behind them. If they stopped, I was upon them. Finally, they decided that they were not going to get any rest that way, so they started marching, single file, back into the pen. They knew all the time where I wanted them to go.

The next day, them little piggies went to the market, and not one of them stayed home. I decided to get out of the pig business and eat roast beef instead.

If those pigs had been horses, I would still be chasing them today. Pigs are smarter than horses. Besides, I saw a pig that could multiply. You know, mathematically, like 2x2 and 2x4. etc.. I have never seen a horse that could do that, but I saw an elephant that could. I also saw an elephant that could dance a jig.

Besides that, I heard about an elephant that could paint pictures. The elephant's owner noticed one day the elephant doodling in the sand with a stick in his trunk. (I guess it was a him, or it might have been a her). The owner gave the elephant a paintbrush and a gallon of paint and said: "OK, paint me some pictures." The elephant started painting and made the owner a fabulous amount of money.

Pigs have more sense than horses and elephants do, too. (In spite of the fact that elephants will work for peanuts and are scared of mice, they are still smarter than horses, and they have a better memory). There are a lot of animals that are smarter than horses. Horses were at the low end of the totem pole when brains were passed out.

What this amounts to is this: I have a theory that explains why the south is considered by other parts of the country to be, you know, dumb. I think that it has something to do with horses and horse sense. In the old days of yore, when cotton was king, The South had a lot of horses and mules (a mule is half horse and half jack ass, not much different). In fact, The South had more horses and mules than any other animals.

There's an old saying that states: "If you lay down with dogs, you will get up with fleas". Another is: "You can judge a person's character by the friends he keeps".
The point I'm trying to make is this: If you keep company with someone, or even with animals for that matter, from sun up to sun down, day after day, year after year, you will take on the

characteristics of that someone or that animal. I know this to be true between people and animals.

Let me give you some examples: Many husbands and wives, that have been married for a long time, look alike, have mannerisms alike, and think like each other. Often times, my wife has read my mind, and sometimes when I didn't want her to. I know that relationships between people and animals can do the same thing.

When I lived in England (I lived there for two years), I had a neighbor that was like her poodle dog. Her voice sounded like the dogs. Her hairstyle was like that of the poodle dog's ears, except for the color. She was a peroxide blonde and the dog was white. She walked like the dog, straddled legged with her hind end sticking out like the poodle's tail, and she wiggled it like the dog wiggled its tail.

Farmers in The Old South, in years gone by, spent more time with their workhorses and mules than they did with people. Therefore, they took on the characteristics of the horses and mules. No one could teach them anything because they had horse sense and were mule headed. Education was a waste of time. Have you noticed that people who claim to have horse sense act like they know everything? If the facts were known, they know very little.

The following are some definitions of people with horse sense:

One lacking in brainpower.

A jackass.

One who wears no socks with his tennis shoes.

One who makes his children pick cotton.

One who wall papers his home with newspapers.

One who uses Sears' catalogs for toilet paper.

One who is too dumb to help his children with homework.

One who was behind the door when brains were meted out.

One whose bed mattress is stuffed with corn shucks.

One who has a two-hole outhouse?

A red neck.

One who is dumber than Charlie McCarthy?

One who thinks the USA's moon landing was a fake.

One who thinks everyone else is dumb.

One whose children are afraid of him.

One who wears a new pair of overalls to funerals?

One who smokes Stud Horse, roll you own, cigarettes and chews Brown's Mule chewing tobacco.

The list can go on and on, but I'm sure you get the gist of it. Let me give you one last example of a person with horse sense:

There was a Sunday school teacher who worked in a cotton mill for thirty years. His job was sweeping and cleaning the water houses (that's what they called the rest rooms). For thirty years he had no other job. He worked the graveyard shift, from mid-night until eight in the morning. He was a teacher in Sunday school. During a class he said and I quote: "Horse sense is more important than a college education". I guess he thought he was the one with the horse sense. Is that funny or what?

That's the way the Old South used to be. It was full with people with horse sense and not much else.

I'm glad horses are gone. I'm glad that I don't have to pick cotton like my daddy did and my granddaddy did.

The South is on the move now. But it will take a while to get rid of all the horse sense and the horse manure that has been used to fertilize the minds of children. Our schools are improving. SAT scores are rising. I see the day coming when the South will be competitive the world over, and will indeed surpass the national average. But it won't be accomplished until we get a broom and sweep all the horse sense and horse manure out the door, and replace it with sound doctrines, academic excellence, good morals, and with parents who care enough to take a hands on interest in their children's education and spiritual development.

You might be wondering what does this horse sense business have to do with building birdhouses? I'm going to tell you and I'm going to be blunt about it: "If all the sense you have is horse sense, don't attempt to build the birdhouses contained in this book. I'm positive that you will get sawdust in your eyes. Then you will grope around blindly and you will end up sawing some of your fingers off. You wouldn't be capable of making a very pretty birdhouse anyway. It would be all lopsided like your personality, and you would blame me"!

So, if all you have is horse sense, go sit down somewhere under a big shade tree and swat the flies and day dream about how smart you are and watch the world pass you by. But if you have a little more ambition than a horse, and if you want to learn, then you can do it. You learn by putting your thoughts to work. You learn by making mistakes, like I have done many times, and by correcting them.

I encourage you to start a hobby that you will enjoy. If I can do it, you can do it. I know what I'm talking about. I'm an electrical engineer by profession. I am retired from the Federal Aviation in Atlanta, Georgia. I was the Southern Region's Airport Lighting Engineer. I had very little experience in carpentry and in wood working when I retired

My first job as a carpenter was that of building a doghouse for my rotweilder, Burt. He was not impressed. He wouldn't go in it. Now,

the dog is gone. I believe some deer hunter shot him, just like they shot another dog I had named Sambo before I got Burt. I found Sambo dead in the woods from a rifle bullet. I brought him home in a wheelbarrow
and buried him outback. Today, the doghouse sits empty in the corner of my backyard.

DOG HOUSE

My next carpentry job was to build a building 20 ft. x 20 ft. with a carport for my pick-up truck. I must say that I did a fair job on the construction of this building, and I enjoyed doing it. I intended to get some shop equipment and piddle around out there seeing what I could do making country things and "do dads".

Well, as soon as I finished the building, my wife took it over. She started making angel dolls, wreaths, and trinkets in it. She was serious about her hobby for a while, but she has, long since, abandoned it. She is now selling Mary K products. She uses the building to store her junk. She does let me use the carport to park my pick-up truck, however.

20 x 20 BUILDING

By the time I got this building finished, I was gaining experience in using a hammer and saw, and I was gaining something else, too - confidence. I actually thought that I could build most anything.

So, I tackled building a barn. I don't have any goats, cows, mules, horses or pigs, but I thought every country home needs a barn. I designed and built a barn all by myself. Now that's confidence for a seventy something year old man, wouldn't you say? But I did it, and a pretty red barn it is, too. The barn is 30 ft x 30 ft x 16 ft high. It has two stories

BARN

After I finished the barn, I didn't know what to do with it. I thought about putting stalls in it and getting some animals, or chickens, or guineas or whatever. But then, who could I get to tend them when I went to visit my seven children and twenty-two grand children? That wouldn't work. I decided to use it as a shop to build birdhouses, birdfeeders, and things.

I have developed this hobby for my pleasure, and like I say to keep occupied. I recommend it for anyone like myself, and for young people, too. If you can build
things faster than me, you could make some money at it. You can do it if you are still able to walk. (I have a bad knee); If you are still able to see (I have cataracts that will require surgery soon); if you can still think straight (my wife asks me sometimes if I have lost my marbles. She knows full well that I haven't had any marbles since I was a boy. I feel like asking her if she has lost her paper dolls. I'll bet she has.)

They tell me that if you don't use something, like an arm or leg, that you will lose the use of it. If exercising your muscles makes your

9

body stronger, and it does, then it just stands to reason that by exercising your brain it will be made stronger. That's why I design and build birdhouses. It has helped me to stay mentally alert (in spite of what my wife may think), and it will help you, also.

I must admit, I was very uncertain whether I had the skills when I built my first birdhouse, and for a long time after the first one. I would change this and change that until I got them like I wanted them. (But, at least, I wasn't like someone I know that starts a hobby and quits). I stayed with it. Now, I can go to town building birdhouses. I enjoy working in my barn. I'm out there almost every day, except for Wednesdays. That's the day I go to the Pickens Jockey Lot. That's another hobby of mine.

FIRST BIRDHOUSE

The birdhouse hobby keeps my mind occupied. I feel that I'm doing something that is interesting and creative. Besides it keeps me out of the house, when all the cleaning, and vacuuming, and Mary K classes are going on. When that's happening, I couldn't nap anyway in my easy chair.

Truthfully, and I'm honest when I say this, I don't build these things expecting to make money. If I did, I would go broke. I would get about a quarter an hour for my labor. I'm slow. Aren't most old men?

It's a good hobby. You should try it. You will be surprised with what you can do.

I have my barn almost full with birdhouses and feeders now, both floors. There are way too many to take to flea markets, yard sells, etc. So, I thought maybe I could get those folks who patronize such places to come to me. I doubt very seriously if I could get many customers to come to the little town of Iva, S. C. just to browse my birdhouses. Sooo.....

I built another building which is 20 ft x 20 ft with a front porch. The reason I built this was because I figured the bigger variety of things that I could offer that more people would come. I plan to use the building to display country things that people like myself, and maybe you, too, like. I haven't decided exactly on all the things that I'm going to build, but you can believe they will be unique and interesting.

If you are down this way, drop in and say howdy. We will be glad to see you, and we may swap some ideas. Two heads are better than one, especially if one of them is old and cranky. But, listen, if you are one of those horse sense fellows, please don't bother to come. You might try to tell me all the things I'm doing wrong, and I wouldn't like that.

Chapter 2

NAMES

NAMES

Parents should ponder long and hard before naming a baby because names are important.

If you have a son and want him to have a shot at becoming president of the United States, give him a name of a former president like John, or George, or Thomas, etc, etc., but leave the former president' s last name off. For example, don't name a son George Washington blank, or Thomas Jefferson_blank. That would be too obvious that you want him to become president and he would never make it.

He would have a better chance if you would just give him the first name of a former president, then send him to Harvard's Law School, and then after he graduates, move next door to CBS News in New York City. He would have a whole lot better shot at becoming president, if you will do that for him.

People associate names with other people they know that have the same names. For instance, I would never name a son of mine Sam, because I know a couple of low class "nerds" who have that name and I certainly wouldn't want my son to grow up to be like them.

Yes, I know, there have been a lot of dignified, well known, Sam's in the world like Uncle Sam, etc, etc, but still, I wouldn't take the chance. My son would have two strikes against him starting out around here with a name like Sam!

Names play a big part in shaping one's personality. If a person is proud of his name, he will likely have a high esteem of himself and more self-confidence. If he doesn't like his name, and is maybe ashamed of his name, he is more likely to become a "weasel." That is, he won't fit in very well with other people.

People with unusual names grow up to be kind of weird. Many of them become college philosophy professors or psychiatrists.

If you don't care about what field of work your son enters in, then give him a name that is hard to spell and pronounce. If you will give him that kind of name, he will probably be able to help psycho nuts when he grows up for he will be one himself.

Girls should have feminine names and graceful names. Never name a pretty little girl, Clyde, or Charlie, or Claude. Those names are for boys.

Many parents want their first child to be a son so bad that when they have a little daughter, they name the little girl the name that they had chosen for a son. Names like that keep many beautiful girls from developing into graceful, feminine ladies.

Girls with boys names get all confused and grow up to join feminist movements such as NOW or some other activist organization. They miss out a lot on pleasures they would have had in just being a wife, and mother, and homemaker. Wouldn't it be much nicer to have a husband to do things that only men can do?

Boys with girls' names grow up in the same manner. They never amount to much. Have you ever heard of a man that is high up the ladder named Doris? Me neither. But some men are named that. Please don't get mad at me if you happen to have a name like that. I know you couldn't help it.

It's just that I think girls should have girl's names and boys should have boy's names. Just like I think men should wear pants and women should wear dresses. (Boy, I hope men don't start wearing dresses. What a revolting development that would be!)

Call me old fashion if you want to, but I know that names have a big effect on a person's personality and happiness in life.

I am also convinced that a lot of the confusion in people's sex lives is caused by having a wrong name. It has to do with the way parents and people relate to names. Some boys and girls become confused, at an early age, as to which sex they belong. Girls want to be boys and boys want to be girls.

Parents should be very careful in choosing names and they should start treating little girl babies like little girls and little boy babies like little boys the day that they are born. I feel that would eliminate some of the confusion and unhappiness concerning sex in our world.

People name pets and animals after people, also, and I think that is wrong. Dogs ought to have names like: Fido, Rover, and Spot, and cats ought to have names like Flossie and Pussy, and Tom (not Thomas).

I'm one of those who don't always practice what I preach because one time we had a mule named Emma. Emma was a good mule. She wasn't mule headed like most mules. She was gentle and calm and easy to plow. She knew what whoa, gee, and haw meant.

Now if I should meet a lady by the name of Emma, I would associate her name with that of our mule, and I would expect her to be gentle and calm and not mule headed. I also would expect her to know what whoa means. Reckon she would?

My son-in-law had a beagle dog that he named Amos, after me. That poor dog didn't stand a chance with a name like that. He got into a lot of fights with dogs that were bigger than he was and they would bite him and chew on his ears.

I believe the reason Amos got into so many fights was because other dogs would make fun of his name and Amos didn't like that. When the other dogs laughed at him and called him names, Amos would pounce on them. He didn't care if they were bigger than he was. Name-calling made him mad (same as it used to do me).

The name, Amos, caused the beagle a lot of confusion, too. Like the times that my son-in-law called him and he wouldn't come because the dog thought he was calling me.

The poor, confused dog finally wandered out into the road and got run over by a woman named Johnny who was driving a big eighteen wheeler. She said she had her mind on other things like politics, running for sheriff, and stuff, and that she just didn't see the dog.

I really don't feel that the world gives enough consideration to names and it started a long time ago. Way back in the Middle Ages, in Europe, people had only one name-- especially in the small villages.

Now, I know that would cause a lot of confusion, especially in the small town of Iva. My mail carrier would never get mail to people with just one name. Many times, he leaves other people's mail in my box that has several names and none of the names even resemble mine. (I wonder if a rural mail carrier has to know how to read? Do you know?)

American Indians thought names and nicknames were important, too. Their names reflect something about their character and personalities and have real significance. Look at some of their names and see if you get the message:

Crow, Sitting Bull, Red Cloud Crazy Horse,
Half Acre, Red Man, Black Foot, Rain Cloud,
Pocahontas (Playful one), Jumping Badger, Crab Tree, Bird Song

Names have been important since the beginning of time. Names in the Bible have real significance: Abraham means, "The Father is high" ...Isaac means: "God laughs"...Israel means, "He strives with God"...David means "Beloved"...Pharaoh means "Great

House"...Isaiah means "Jehovah has saved" and Peter means "Petros or Rock".

Some other names and their meanings are: Amos "courage"...Arthur "bold and brave"...Ava "filled with grace"...Benjamin "mighty in spirit"...Charles "strong and manly...Clyde "warm, loving spirit"...Denise "favored one"...Edna "vigorous one"...George "land worker, farmer"...Imogene "blessed one"...John "God is generous".

Nicknames describe people's physical characteristics, or the opposite, sometimes. Many nicknames develop by contraction of names and by use of pet, personal, nicknames. Let's look at some examples:

Stretch...A six foot six inch fellow who weighs 130 pounds.
Scratch...One who scratches himself all the time.
Tiny...A big fat guy.
Dynamite...A puny, skinny guy.
Stick...A fellow lame in one leg and walks with a crutch.
Lightning...A guy slower than a turtle.
Fossil...A classmate thought he looked like one and it stuck.
Radio...A girl that talks all the time.
One Eye...An unfortunate fellow who had only one eye.
Four eyes...A fellow way back yonder when not many wore glasses.
Shorty...He was about 5 feet tall.
Dumb Dumb...Coach Frank Howard thought he was too dumb to be one person.
Penguin...A baseball player that walked like a penguin.
Butter Beans...A 300 pound boxer that would probably get the butter beans beat out of him by a fly weight if he could dance real good.
Sugar...A boxer who was not very sweet.
Smiley...A fellow that owns a cafe and makes a lot of money.
Pig...A guy who has a pug nose and looks like a pig
Black Boy...A white man with a tan complexion.
Boog...A lady whose name was Notburga.
Refrigerator...A Chicago Bears football player.
Too Tall...A Dallas Cowboys football player.
Ike...A little boy named Isaac.
Ank...An old man named Amos

Dub...A fellow whose mama called him "W.T."
Big Mildred. She was 'sho nough' big!
Cubby...He looked like a teddy bear.
Half Pint...A comrade who is always a half pint low.
Nub... A one and half arm painter who said he always started from the bottom.
Pigmy...A short football player for old Iva High.

Yes, names and nicknames are important. Parents should be very careful in selecting names. If the names are wrong, they can do a lot of damage to one's personality and cause a lot of misery. For these reasons I tried to be very careful in naming my birdhouses. I, like most people, probably messed up a time or two, but I did the best I could. I realize there's something about names that make things unique. See if you agree with the names that I have selected for my birdhouses. I hope you will find the descriptions interesting and informative.

Chapter 3

BIRDHOUSES

AND

BIRDFEEDERS

DUTCH TWEET

When I was a young GI in Europe during World War II, my outfit was given a rest of two weeks from the rigors of war. We were sent to Venlo, Holland. Dutch civilians opened their homes to us. I and another soldier, by the name of Capps, stayed with a nice young couple that had a small baby. My other comrades were dispersed to homes next door and across the street.

The Dutch were very, very nice to us. Living so close (almost like part of the family), we became intimately acquainted.

If I had not been so bashful, I stood a good chance of really making friends with a girl next door by the name of Lydia. She was beautiful, too, with long blonde hair and pretty blue eyes. She was gorgeous.

When our time was up, the Dutch gave us a going away party. And this glamorous lady literally lassoed me and pulled me out onto the dance floor. I almost croaked! That was the very first time in my life that I had tried to dance (I only did it then because I couldn't find a hole to crawl into and hide). Only one dance was all I could muster though she persistently tried to get me to dance again.

Well, after the party, I and most of my comrades went back to our host's homes for our last night with them. About 2 or 3 in the morning, there was a knock on my door. It was two brothers of that beautiful blonde. They wanted to now if I had seen Lydia. She had not come home. Another hour went by and she finally showed up...with Capps. They had taken the long way home.

According to Capps, they had been sitting on a park bench talking. For three hours??? Yeah, that's what Capps said, and do you know what?? I believed him. He was dumb enough to do something like that.

I don't know why the Dutch have a reputation of being stubborn. They were not nearly as stubborn as some Southerners I know that think they know everything. You know the ones I'm talking about – the ones who think they have horse sense – the ones that disagree with about everything you say. If it's cloudy and looks like rain and you say, "Well, I believe we might get a shower of rain to-day". They will say; "Naw, it's not going to rain. In order for it to rain the wind must blow from the West. It's blowing from the East today". (Or some other stupid remark like that.) There used to be a lot of those types around in the South; but the South is getting better. You don't find as many like that today. We are more congenial, like I found the Dutch to be.

There used to be mean ones, too, in the South. If you had been out with their sister and brought her home at three in the morning, her brother would have knocked your "block" off. The Dutch didn't do Capps that way. They just shook his hand and told him goodnight.

I guess that there are good people all over the world – even in Afghanistan, Iran, and Iraq. And there are probably some "bad eggs" in every country, also.

I really feel that people, the world over, are getting better and that there are not nearly as many mean ones now as we had when I was a boy.

I think the reason people are getting better is that the world is getting smaller. We have computers that can zip e-mail from one continent to another in a few seconds flat, and jet airplanes that can fly around the world in a couple of days, and international games of competition. People are getting acquainted the world over. Maybe the day is coming when people of all races and colors will shake hands and be friends. I hope so.

Anyway, take my word for it. The Dutch are good people. They really gave us GI's a Dutch tweet". I mean "Dutch treat".

ONE-EYED JOE

There were a lot more One-eyed Joes in the old days than today. The reasons? Times were tougher, people were meaner and doctors were dumber back then.

Most things that make life safer and easier were invented in the last seventy years. Things like: chain saws, bulldozers, ditch diggers, cat scans, laser beams, computers, and on and on.

In the old days, people had to work for a living - from the time it got light enough to see until it got so dark that you couldn't see.

Back then everything was done by hand (and mule), from digging ditches, building roads, or baling hay; consequently, people sweat a lot, smelled a lot (that was before deodorant), and they attracted a lot of flying insects - especially gnats!

If you lived in the South and worked and sweated and smelled, and you didn't know how to pucker your lips just right and blow the gnats away, they would get in your eyes and cause you misery.

There were a lot of One-eyed Joes walking around back then that got that way because they didn't blow the gnats away. Gnats got in their eyes and gave them "red-runny" sore eyes.

The nearest doctor was about thirty miles away (a two day trip by mule and wagon). So, people had to make do with what they had – in other words, they used home remedies like cloverine salve, turpentine, iodine, etc. Some of the things they used were not suitable for sore eyes. (Ask some old One-eyed Joes. They know.) Times were tough back then.

Another thing back then, many boys didn't get to go to school much. They were needed on the farm – especially on the farms in the mountains. They tell me that some of those mountaineer farmers could get twenty gallons of "White-lightning"
per acre of corn.

"White Lightning" was the favorite drink of the men in the old South – especially on Saturdays.

"White Lightning" was firewater – 100-proof firewater! Men who drank it got their bellies on fire. Their eyes bulged out (and made good targets in a fist fight). Their faces got red. Their speech got blurred so bad that they couldn't even talk Southern style – and they got mean. They came to town on Saturdays looking for a fight. Since there were a lot of other characters just like them in town, in the same mood, they got what they were looking for!

A lot of One-eyed Joes down South blame their condition on getting hit with a ten-pound fist in the eye while they were mean with "White Lightning"!!

Lastly, another reason that there were more One-eyed Joes in the old days than there are today is because the doctors were dumber back then. They didn't know much more about treatments than did the parents.

I've got cataracts today in both eyes. I'm sure glad that doctors have wised up and know how to remove them.

I would hate to be a One-eyed Joe like my uncle because some doctor put my eye out! That's what my uncle said a doctor did to him in the old days.

You hardly ever see a One-eyed Joe today and I am glad!!

BARN OWL BOARDING HOUSE

During farming season, our barn was used as a dwelling place for mules. We put them in a pasture during winter. The barn also housed something else-owls, snakes, rats, and cats. (All kinds of stuff).

I know it had owls in it because one sat on a fence post looking at me with its big round eyes, one night when I brought Mama home from the mill (she still worked in the mill. I learned to drive at the age of sixteen so that I could take her there and fetch her back. She tried to learn to drive, but she went through a barbed wire fence, and she would never try it again.)

I know the barn had snakes because I turned a log over in it and a copper head was under it. I ran back and picked up a rock about the size of your fist and threw it at the snake. When the rock was about 3 feet from the snake, the snake struck the rock, and BINGO, the rock bashed the snake's head against the log, and the snake was dead. (I learned to throw rocks like that by rock battling with my two older brothers, Richard and "Dub". When they wanted to go somewhere and didn't want me tagging along, they would throw rocks at me to drive me back home...and of course, I would return their fire).

I know the barn had cats because one had kittens in the loft. My brother, John, decided to move the kittens to a safer place. He climbed up into the loft and was handing the kittens down to me below and I was putting them in a box...When suddenly, John fell out of the loft onto my back and sent me flying into the box with the kittens. I started to beat him up, but then, I thought: "the clumsy ox couldn't help it, so I let him go".

I guarantee you the Barn Owls in that barn had plenty to eat like: fat rats, big snakes, and maybe a kitten now and then (do owls eat kittens?). Anyway, whatever owls like most, I'm sure they found it in that barn. It was a good boarding house for them (but the holes in my birdhouse may be too small for them. If they are fat, they will need big holes).

Barn Owls, with those great big round eyes, have telescopic vision. That is, they can see in the dark. (Well almost dark). That is why they are night hunters.

And another thing, do you think they can turn their heads three hundred and sixty degrees around? They look like they do, but, I think that's a myth; but, I'm sure they can turn their heads further than I can. I can only turn my head about ninety degrees before my neck starts hurting.
Maybe you young folks can turn your head further, like a Barn Owl, and maybe you are night hunters, too. A lot of young folks are today – with their "souped-up" Camaros, Trans Ams, etc. You see them prowling around every Friday and Saturday nights at the malls, looking this way and that (like Barn Owls), with beams in their eyes, looking for prey (good looking "chicks" without escorts).

When I was a teenager, we had to be in by dark and get a good night's sleep so we would be ready to go hoe cotton by sun up.

Barn Owls, snakes and young male teenagers have a lot in common –
they are all "kinda" sneaky!!

Barn Owls, to me, look spooky. (I'll bet they hypnotize their prey, too
– just staring at the prey, without blinking, for long periods of time).
That's the way hypnotists do it. They stare at you, with half closed
eyes, and maybe hold a swaying object before you and say in a
monotone voice: "you are getting sleepy – so….oo…oo sleepy" and
sure 'nough, you might find yourself dozing off – going under the
spell – before you know it.

Do you know if Barn Owls use hypnosis? I think they do!

EGRET'S HANGOUT

My house is on a hill and I have a good view of a stream from my kitchen window. Surrounding the stream are willows and reeds and rushes - a good hiding place for all sorts of things like frogs, lizards, tadpoles, and maybe some water snakes. (things that Herons and Egrets like).

There are two long legged creatures, one white and the other gray, that hangout down there. I think they are Egrets. I can't get close enough to be sure, but I think that's what they are. I know that Herons are bluish in color (aren't they?).

These birds must have a nest close by because they don't seem to fly very well. Every time I see them in the air, they are just swooping in for a landing with their legs tucked in close to their bellies and straight out behind them (like they might have just come sailing out a nearby tree).

If they see me, they make a funny sound like a barn door squeaking on rusty hinges and they slowly flop their wings and fly away.

They are beautiful birds with plumes starting between their shoulder blades and going past their tails. Women and foreign generals used to wear these plumes. But since women have quit wearing hats with plumes and foreign generals, too, the Egrets are making a comeback.

Egrets and Herons, like a lot of other birds, are waders. (I was a wader once myself, until I learned how to swim). Even though it seems a zillion years ago, I remember how I learned to swim. We boys dammed up a creek with sand bags (Guano burlap sacks with sand in them). When the water got to be about "belly button" deep, we took off our clothes and jumped in. I remember I couldn't swim, so I just kept my feet on the bottom and would give myself a push and pretended that I was swimming. Sometimes I could push myself through the water, without my feet touching the bottom, maybe for eight or ten feet. I kept doing that, pushing and kicking and moving my arms, until I learned how to swim.

But, Egrets are waders – not swimmers. God made them that way, with their long, skinny legs, so that they could go wading in ponds, and catch minnows, tadpoles, lizards, etc. (Egrets, also have long spear shaped bills with which to catch their prey – isn't nature wonderful?).

In the old days; (days of my youth) we used to go swimming at Burris's Mill. That was a corn mill located on Wilson's Creek. Mr. Burris built a dam across the creek, using timbers and planks. (He put bobbed wire on the planks of the dam to keep us boys from jumping up and down on his dam, which could have caused the dam to leak).

He built a waterway from the dam to the corn mill house (out of lumber also). The water going down this chute had quite a fall from the dam to the corn mill house – enough fall to turn a huge water wheel, which rotated big stones for grinding corn into meal.

The water that turned the water wheel returned to the creek below the dam. You would often see Egrets and other wading birds under the water wheel - I guess that was a good feeding place and safe hiding place for them.

30

WOOD WARBLER'S CABIN

Have you heard a bird singing a tune, while in flight, that sounded a bit like someone
drumming on an old banjo? That was a Bobolink of the Wood Warbler family.

Have you seen a bird with a bright orange-yellow head and breast with a black beak and with light gray wings? That's another Wood Warbler. Actually its real name is Prothonotry Warbler. It is found in swampy places of the Southeast. That's the one this birdhouse is intended for. The Prothonotary Warbler is an excellent flycatcher.

The South has a hot humid climate in the summer and the swamps are thick with vegetation, flying insects, stinging insects, mosquitoes, and flies – things that Wood Warblers like.

It would be ok with me if the beautiful Prothonotary Warbler would catch (and eat) all those things. Then they wouldn't be around to bite and pester my Louisiana friends when they go fishing and crawdadding down on the bayous.

Have you ever eaten any crawdads? I think that's what I ate one time in New Orleans

fixed Cajun style (yummy delicious). I tried to get my wife to steal their recipes, but she said there's a scarcity of crawdads around here. I guess I will have to move to Louisiana. Just kidding. The crawdads are good, but I couldn't stand all that jazz. I will just have to be content with visiting at Mardi gras time. I like those parades. Have you been? It's fun (Mister, throw me some beads)

Anyway, male Wood Warblers are often like the displays on the floats in Mardi Gras Parades – brilliantly colored.

Most Wood Warblers are brightly colored – both male and female; but the males often "out shine" the females (isn't that something?). The male's bright array of colors attract the females "kinda" like the way girls and ladies are attracted to guys who own Mercedes and BMW convertibles!

Another way that some Wood Warblers resemble ladies of today is with their toes and claws. Wood Warblers toes and claws are longer today than they used to be. Don't you agree that ladies toenails and fingernails are longer today than they used to be? (And they paint them, too, where people will surely notice them.) I saw one lady in church that had extended her nails with brightly colored plastic ones. "Yeah", and I admit they were pretty; but (wow!) I would hate the thoughts of keeping them pretty.

I'm glad men don't worry about painting their toenails and fingernails and keeping them pretty – I'm afraid I wouldn't attract very many females, if I had to do that!!

Another thing about Wood Warblers, a few of the Northern variety of Wood Warblers are not nearly as pretty. Some are dark in color, both male and female, the year round.

Bird watchers go nuts trying to tell the males and females apart. (Like it is for us sometimes to tell the boys from the girls.) But, I'm glad Wood Warblers do come in a variety of colors.

My wife and I like to go to the mall, sometimes, on Saturday night and watch the parade – the parade of teenagers and young people. They come in all sizes, shapes, and colors – some with waxed hairdos – some with the seats of their pants down to their knees – some with clocks (I'm talking about wall clocks, hanging around their necks) – some in tuxedos – some in short – short (I'm talking about "shore 'nough" short) shorts. I'm telling you the "Mardi Gras Parade" doesn't compare with the parade you see sometimes at malls on Saturday nights.

The Wood Warblers in all their variety of colors, have nothing on our teenagers of today (even if bird watchers do have trouble sometimes of telling the males from the females).

PAPA'S POUT HOUSE

I don't mind seeing pretty little girls pout. I think they look cute when they stick out their bottom lip, and make them quiver to make you have pity. (That's the way my daughter, Maggie, used to pout when she wanted something special, when she was little); but I don't like to be around pouting grown women. The silence "bugs" me. Especially ..... especially if I don't even know why they are pouting (which is often the case with those who like to pout). They don't have to have a reason. They will pout just because their husbands haven't noticed that they have been wearing the same dress to church for the last three Sundays, (such little things that don't amount to a "hill of beans").

I understand that most women pout. (There must be something in their hormones that make them do that). But, men don't pout. When their wives make them mad, men just go out and slam the door, kick the dog, and have a "snort" or two or three of booze.

That's what my Papa would do when Mama said something he didn't like. He would head to his little Pout House, where he kept his bottle

34

of booze. After a while, he would come back, lit up like a Christmas tree, and just as happy as he could be. He had forgotten all about what Mama said that had made him mad. "Shoot" Papa wouldn't pout...even though he had a Pout House.

Setting hens pout. The reason they pout, I think, is because they don't want those high-spirited, macho, red roosters bothering them. The hens are not in a romantic mood while they are setting on eggs and trying to raise a family. So, they pout and squawk when they get off the nest to take a short break.

Nobody enjoys being around pouting and squawking females – not even macho red roosters. Come to think of it, maybe that's the reason a lot of women pout and squawk is that they don't want to be pestered by their macho husbands. (Hey, I hope you don't think that this is the voice of experience talking. My wife really doesn't pout and I'm not really – really macho!)

But, I had rather be alone on the banks of some lake or river than to be in a house with a pouting and squawking woman, wouldn't you? (Maybe that's the reason the world has so many fishermen. Don't you agree?) And, that might be the reason why there are so many moose hunters, bear hunters, and crocodile hunters - have you seen that guy on television that wrestles and captures crocodiles? It's unreal how he snares those crocodiles with his bare hands, and the crocodiles biting and snapping at him all the time. I'll bet he has a pouting, squawking wife at home! Well, something has driven him to be so brave. If it's not a pouting, squawking wife then what is it? (It might be the IRS – I know that some moose hunters in Alaska went there trying to escape the threats and pursuits of the IRS). Some people will do anything to escape – even wrestle a bear or a crocodile.

I saw where the brother of the guy, Rudolf that has been accused of bombing abortion clinics sawed off his hand on a table saw. The reason he sawed off his hand was because the FBI wouldn't leave him alone, pestering him with questions about the "where abouts" of his brother. (He had all he could take of the FBI nagging him, so, he sawed off his hand)!

Gosh, I hope that I am never pestered with such things as pouting women, the IRS, or the FBI to the extent that I would leave good "ole" Iva, South Carolina. I'm going to hang around here as long as I can.

In Iva, men don't pout. Only little girls, a few women, and setting hens pout – and I'm glad!

SEE ROCK CITY

You used to see "See Rock City" birdhouses everywhere, but you don't see them much anymore. I guess it's because almost everyone has seen Rock City. But frankly, I haven't seen it. Furthermore, I don't have much desire to see it. Oh I have no doubts that it must be an unusual city. It's just that I have seen enough rock in my lifetime.

I remember one time, a long time ago, when I was coming home from school; I stubbed my big toe on a rock sticking up out of the ground. It stubbed all the skin off, and it hurt so bad that I just sat down on the ground and cried (even though I was by myself and my mama couldn't hear me, I cried). You couldn't blame me though because I was just a little ole bare footed boy of about seven.

Another time, when I was playing with rocks, trying to see how far up in the air I could throw them, one came down and hit me in the back of the head. Wow, did that hurt. I saw stars, Jupiter, Mars, and Pluto, all of them. I still have a scar in the back of my head where that rock landed. No hair will grow there. I have a time brushing my hair to cover the scar where the ladies won't notice it.

Another thing, you could have gathered enough rock off the farm that I lived on to build a rock city. (Maybe that's how Rock City got built). Some farmer got tired of plowing in the rocks, and he just gathered up all the rocks and built a city and started charging people to see it. That would beat the "heck" out of farming in rocky ground.

It's no fun to be plowing along when suddenly your plow hits a big rock. Somebody can get hurt that way. Ask me. I know, for it has happened to me more than once. And if you have never chopped cotton, bare footed, in rocky ground, you don't know what fun you have been missing.

We have a river nearby that is named "Rocky River". Before they dammed this river up and made Lake Succession out of it, we used to ride our "bikes" down there and go fishing and swimming and camping out.

On one of these expeditions, we were diving into the river (some boys from limbs of trees above the river and some from the river bank).

I climbed a tree and really made a "belly whopper". When I came up, I was near the bank and there was a big rock protruding out over the river. I cut a big gash in my butt on this rock. It hurt and bled and it kept me from having fun like I was having that day.

As far as I was concerned the "mud cats" and "horny heads" and "suckers" could have their hiding places under those rocks. I wouldn't disturb them again.

I'm glad they dammed the river up and made Lake Succession. People come from all over to visit the lake. There's some of the best fishing in Lake Succession that you will find in most fresh water lakes in the South-bass and crappie and bream and even cat fish (I like cat fish, don't you? With french-fries and hush puppies and cold slaw and country ham – yummy)!

Now, do you understand why I don't want to see Rock City? I've seen enough rocky and hard places in my life. I've got it made now. I just want to sit back and enjoy the finer things of life that God has made – like the beautiful birds; cool - clear waters, daffodils peeping through the snow – nature. I can see that God's hand made it <u>all,</u> and I do enjoy it. Don't you?

A HOME IN THE STICKS

There is one thing that I will never understand and that is: Why did they used to build houses, up until about the 40's, high off the ground, often with rocks as pillars, without any underpinning?? Most houses, especially country homes, were built this way (and, brother, they were cold in the winter time).

The house we lived in, way out in the sticks, was like that. We heated the living area with a wood-burning fireplace. The rest of the house didn't have any heat except for the kitchen's wood stove at cooking time. If you got three feet from the fireplace, you would freeze to death.

We boys slept in our union suits (that's what they called long johns back then) with about four heavy quilts in beds with feather mattresses. Our beds were cozy enough, but it was cold when we got out of them on the cold winter mornings. We would jump out of bed, jump in our frozen stiff overalls, and dash for the fire that my daddy had already built. (BRR!!) It gives me chills just thinking about it).

Most of the country roads were dirt. I mean red mud. A driver had to stay in the ruts or he would wind up in a ditch (all the ditches on the sides of the roads were deep).

Our house was located about four miles down one of these muddy roads. Even though I lived way out in the sticks, I played high school basketball and had to walk home most nights after we played. But one rainy, down pouring, night after an away game, my coach told the bus driver to take me home before he took the other players back to town. Well, the bus driver made it down that muddy road and around the curves and got me safely home. But, on the way back, he got out of the ruts and the bus slid into a deep ditch. All the boys had to get out and help push the bus out. They told me about it the next day, what an ordeal that was with the rain pouring down. They got mud all over those "hand-me-down" uniforms (our school was poor, too, just like we were).

People had to put up with a lot of hardships back then, especially if you lived in the sticks.

Times were hard back then – not only for my family, but also for most families. (Even our schools were heated with coal burning heaters.)

Teachers had to live in boarding houses. (And, I'm telling you some of those houses were pitiful – kerosene heaters – no plumbing –out houses, etc. etc.). But, we had the best teachers in the world! They were dedicated, committed, called by God to teach. And they loved us "little ole", "shaggy headed", ragged, barefooted country boys and girls. (If it had not been for my teachers in my boyhood days, I believe I would still be living in the sticks in a house, maybe with cracks in the floor, and with a wood fire as the main source of heat).

Life is better today. We have come a long way – especially the South. We don't suffer the hardships that our fathers and forefathers went

41

through. The reason we don't have to suffer like they did is because of one word – "education".

I give credit to my early teachers for inspiring me to get an education. If you happen to be a poor, unloved, suffering young person, reading this book, please let me give you a piece of sound advice; "get an education". It will take discipline (self discipline). It will take commitment (total commitment). It will take long hours of study and hard work; but, the rewards will be great. The opportunities are there. Don't be satisfied with living in "A Home In The Sticks" when you can have a mansion in the sky.

Today, the sky is the limit for birds, airplanes, missiles, and for young people with ambition! "A Home In The Sticks" is for the birds!

TIN LIZZY

I know that most of you people are way too young to know what a "Tin Lizzy" is. A "Tin Lizzy" is a "T" Model Ford, which was built in the '20's. I guess the reason it got the nickname "Tin Lizzy" is because some influential person or people (like Hollywood) called it that and it stuck.

Believe me (I'm that old) the car was not made out of tin. It was made out of steel, which was much thicker than the cars of today.

The "Tin Lizzy" had something else that you don't find on cars today. It had a high voltage coil.

There was a cotton mill grease monkey in Iva that loved to tinker with "T" models. One day, he called me over to his "T" model which was putt putting along in idle. When I came up to him, he put one hand on the car and the other on my right ear. That crazy fool sent an electrical shock through my ear, down my side, through my leg and bare foot to

43

the ground. I yelled and jumped sky high. I never trusted that jerk again.

I don't know what kind of birds will build in the "Tin Lizzy", but if you put it near the back porch, I'll bet it will be wrens. They like back porches.

DOBBIN'S BRIDGE

"Put on your old gray bonnet with the blue ribbons on it ... while I hitch Old Dobbin to the shaves ... and to the fields of clover we will ride all over... on our golden wedding day". That's an oldie - older than even me. Someone down South has changed it a bit and put in "cotton" instead of "clover" and put in "we will go a trotting" instead of "we will ride all over". Even this version is older than the hills and most of you have never had the pleasure of hearing either version sung (that's the reason I sang it here. Hope you enjoyed it).

Old Dobbin, of course, was a horse (might have been a mule. But horses were used most of the time to pull buggies).

People went courting in buggies back then instead of convertibles, with the top laid back, like we did when I was courting (course I didn't have a convertible, but my buddy did. That's the reason he was my buddy).

Those covered bridges were used by farmers back then to stop under when it was raining as they were coming from town with their week's supply of groceries; or maybe they were used by boys (like me when I was a boy) to climb on and to jump into the creek and have fun; or maybe they were used by sweethearts for a Sunday's buggy ride. I wish covered bridges could talk. I'll bet what they would have to say would be interesting.

Dobbins Bridge, which is the name of this bird feeder, was taken from a covered bridge by that name located in Anderson County, South Carolina.

There were other covered bridges in our area existing at the time that I was a boy (I remember traveling through several of them), but, of course, that's been long ago and covered bridges have long since been torn down and replaced with new and wider concrete bridges.

People don't travel much anymore by horse and buggy, or by mules and wagons, or by bobbed-tailed horses and sleighs; consequently covered bridges are not needed today.

We are in a big hurry today to get to our destination as fast as we can. We don't have time to stop and smell the roses, honeysuckles, tulips, and wild flowers like the "old timers"!

I think, maybe, with all our gadgets, and cars, and trains, and jet planes that we are living too fast.

Don't get me wrong. I don't think that life was better back in the days of horses and buggies and covered bridges. (Man, I wouldn't want to go back to those days for anything in the world). It's just that, in our present world, we live so fast that we don't take time to visit, and chat, and get acquainted with our neighbors like our fathers and grandfathers did.

It's true that covered bridges are not needed today; but, I think it would be wonderful if we could recapture the genuine spirits that existed during the era of covered bridges – you know the spirit of "loving thy neighbor as thyself" – the spirit of "children obey your parents"—the spirit of "marriage until death do us part": -- the spirit of trust and honesty when no one bothered to lock their doors.

Dobbins Bridge is more than a covered bridge. This bridge is a symbol of by-gone days --an era of our founding fathers -- an era of brotherly love.

PROSPECTOR'S CABIN

There are a lot of prospectors in Alaska. They go there for different reasons. Some go there to escape alimony payments. Others go there because they like the wilds. Others go there to make a bundle (they have heard that there is gold in"dem dar" hills).

I went there because my boss, the US Army Corps of Engineers, thought it would be a good idea if I went (Alaska needed engineers to help them get their utilities restored after the great earthquake).

I almost became a full-fledged "sour dough" while I was there. I met two of the three requirements. I peed in the Yukon River and I wrestled a grizzly bear, but I didn't sleep with an Eskimo squaw. That I did not do. I was married and I decided it would be best if I just remained a down under 48 dude.

There are a lot of tough nuts in Alaska (besides the mooses). One was a hermit prospector who lived in a cabin way back in the wilds. He saw two geologists on the side of a mountain one day who were looking for oil. The old prospector came down the mountain to where they were. They were the first human beings that he had seen in two years. His first words were: "Gimme a tailor-made cigarette"

The two geologists were back up there a year later and he approached them again and said: "Gimme a tailor-made cigarette". They asked him: "Do you live up here all by yourself? Don't you have any neighbors?" He said: "I used to have a neighbor who lived on another mountain about twenty miles, as the crow flies. He would drop by to see me every year or so. but I had not seen him in a long, long time, so I hiked over to his mountain and I found him dead in bed. He had been dead for a long time for he was just a skeleton". That's the price that some of those old prospectors have to pay. They live alone and they die alone.

There was another old prospector up there that carried a beat up old leather brief case with him. The brief case was crammed full with stuff. Each item in it had a history. He was showing me all his stuff, old broken knives, bear teeth, Eskimo pouches, etc., and he pulled out a dry, shriveled up, index finger. I said: "where in the world did you get that?" He said: "I was by a saw mill one day and a fellow sawed his finger off, so I just picked it up and threw it in the brief case".

Alaska has a lot of old prospectors and trappers who spend months and months out in the wilderness alone. Seldom do they come to town. When they do come to town, (maybe once in a "blue moon"), they get drunk and party and blow the money they got for the gold dust and furs and back to the wilderness they go. What a rugged life they live! (And cold---I mean so cold that ice cycles form in their beards and eyebrows)---well it takes all types of people to make the world go'round! If we all liked the same things this would be a dull world, wouldn't it?

Another experience I had in Alaska: I applied for a room at a motel in Anchorage (I think the name of it was the Roosevelt Motel). The clerk at the desk said she could let me have a room. I asked her if I could look at the room before I checked in. She gave me a key and I went to

the room. There was another person's gear in the room – boots, backpack, clothes and fishing gear. I returned to the clerk and told her "there is another man's belongings in the room". She said "certainly, you don't think you can have a room for yourself alone, do you?"
.

Alaska is still wild. I mean by that: Alaska has not been tamed. There are wild animals galore in Alaska and Alaska has attracted a lot of wild people – untamed people (I mean besides the Eskimos and Indians). You see them walking around with pistols strapped to their sides, (like the wild – wild West used to be)

Alaska is the last frontier, and a lot of tough untamed prospectors have gone there to conquer it (like the Pilgrims conquered the wilds of America). I believe they will succeed, don't you?

WHIP-POOR-WILL TOWN HOUSE

Before you say anything, I have a confession to make;" I misnamed this birdhouse. But it's one of the last ones I made, and I'm tired and I didn't want to take time and go back and rename it".

It's misnamed because you know and I know that a whip-poor-will is not going to live in town. Whip-poor-wills are country birds. They like it in the sticks. The further back in the woods and thickets, the better they like it. I know this from experience.

I was clearing some land with a bulldozer (that's another thing that I learned to do since I retired, and you could too, if you tried). I was operating way back in the thickets, on a creek, in bottomland, where honeysuckles, muscadine vines, hedges, brush, and big poplar trees had taken over. It was dark back in there, even though it was daylight and the sun was shining outside. Suddenly, this big, strange, brave bird came swooping down out of a tree and almost knocked my hat off. It scared the daylights out of me. I started to get off my bulldozer

51

and run for cover, the way I did one time when yellow jackets got after me, but I stayed put this time, and watched to see if this weird creature would attack me again.

It lit on a limb and watched me for a while. Finally, I guess it decided that I wasn't going to leave so it flew off. You don't often get a good look at a whip-poor-will, for they only come out when it's getting dark, but I did that day.

Birds will attack people like that. My wife said mocking birds attacked her. She was going to the mail box and she said mocking birds swooped down and tried to peck her (actually, I think they were attacking her cat that was walking with her. They don't like cats).

Some killdeers attacked a buddy of mine, John Naglish. He used to work with me when I worked with the FAA. He was on a field trip and killdeers dived bombed him. Got it all over his nice, clean, white shirt. Hey, if you see John, don't say anything about this because it makes him mad. He likes to be in control and that little bird showed him who was in control that day.

Some birds are born mean. They will fight each other - Hummingbirds; they will attack people and cats – Mockingbirds and Blue Jays; some will peck on the gutters of your house just to annoy you – red headed Woodpeckers; some will build nests on your porch light fixtures – Barn Swallows; and some will come around your house at night (especially if you live in the country like me) and hoot at you – Hoot Owls and Whip-poor-wills.

As for me, I like to hear the sounds of birds. I like to hear the Bluebirds chirping as they sit on the electric lines coming to my house. And to hear Barn Swallows make sweet, tweet-tweet, sounds are good for my ears. I like to hear the sounds of Blue Jays that go: "jay, jay, jay bird" or something like that. And, I like to hear Old Crows (especially when something excites them); I even like to hear the sounds of Whip-poor-wills as they come around at night when lights go on in my house. I'm just an "ole" country boy at heart and

Whip-poor-wills are country birds. They sing a tune that is music to my heart.

But, my brother, Alvin, doesn't like the sounds of all the birds like I do. He especially doesn't like to hear the sounds of Crows in his corn patch (He's still a farmer). And, He doesn't like to hear the sounds of Whip-poor-wills that light in the trees across the street from his house and sing to him when it begins to get dark. He shoots at them.

The poor birds don't know why Alvin shoots at them. The birds feel that Alvin is the intruder – not them. Who is right? I vote for the birds. They were here before he came. Right?

EGGING IT ON

Egging it on, among other things, I guess means: to insight, to resist, to stand your grounds, and I'm sure it might mean some other things.

But, do you know how this phrase originated? I'm not sure, but I feel that it had something to do with eggs. You know, the raw, uncooked kind, the slimy ooey kind.

I feel like the phrase might have started way back yonder, maybe in the Roman days, when Nero was emperor of Rome.

Here's my theory, but please don't quote me on it: Maybe, when Nero was the emperor, he confiscated all the Christians' weapons - their swords, their slings, their bows and arrows, everything that they had with which they could fight and defend themselves. All that they had left was some hen eggs, duck eggs and goose eggs.

The word got out in the Christian community that Nero was going to be riding, in his open chariot, down the cobbled stone streets of Rome on the morrow at the tenth hour. Messengers were sent out to urge all able bodied Christians to assemble themselves to be along the streets at the appointed hour with well filled baskets of raw eggs and to give the emperor a good pelting in retaliation for all the miseries that he had caused them.

Well, the Christians turned out in big numbers. Many had baskets, and many others just came to watch the fun. Such a clamor of folks you have never seen. The streets were full of people.

When the Emperor showed up, you wouldn't believe the pelting he got. Of course some of the Christians couldn't throw too good (especially the women folks, they had glass arms), and eggs were splattered everywhere - all over the Emperor's uniform, all over the many medals on his chest, in his beard, and all over his face. The Christians were surely angry with him and they let him have it! They really egged it on His Royal Highness.

When Nero saw all the slime on his pure bred horses and on his lovely chariot, and when he felt the ooey slime trickle down his cheeks, he went stark raving mad! He stopped his chariot then and there, and he ordered his army to set fire to Rome. And while the city burned, he took out his fiddle and sat there on the curb, with egg all over him, and played, at a very rapid pace; "THERE'S GONNA BE A HOT TIME IN THE OLD TOWN TO-NIGHT!!!"

From that time on the Emperor was a "mad man". He sent his troops out to the Christian communities to arrest all the people they could find that were responsible for the "Egging On" that he received.

They brought Christians back to Roman Coliseums by the trainloads (I mean by wagon loads).

He threw the Christian boys and girls and women into the lion's dens, and he made the Christian men fight gladiators who were on horseback, who had sharp swords and spears. The Christian men had nothing – only their bare hands.

Great throngs of Nero's subjects flocked to the coliseums to watch the slaughter of Christians by the Roman gladiators (similar to the throng of Clemson fans that come to watch the slaughter of the Carolina

Gamecocks by Clemson in football games) such cheering you have never heard the likes!!!

Nero sat in his isolated, royal booth and ranted and raved and cheered his gladiators on! You could hear his voice above all the crowd: "go gladiator go! Fight – fight – fight!!" He would yell at the top of his lungs!! Yes, Nero burned the town and slaughtered Christians by the hundreds in retaliation for the "Egging on Him" that he got that day. How sad that was!

Anyway, that's my theory about how the phrase "Egging It On" got started. Don't you think my theory is reasonable??

OVER THE MOON

I know that there ain't no cow agile enough to jump over the real moon that's up in the sky. So I guess the nursery rhyme is talking about a different kind of moon (like maybe in Moonie). Now I know that there are cows that could jump over this kind of moon.

My brother, Alvin, had a 2000-pound Black Angus bull that could jump that high. He jumped over a four-foot high barbed wire fence several times to get with the neighbor's cows. My brother decided he couldn't allow that (the neighbor might not want half black angus calves and half something else). So he built an electric fence a few feet in front of the barbed wire fence. The next time the bull started to jump the fence, his leg touched the electric fence. He let out a bellow, and rolled his eyes back into his head until nothing but white was showing, and he snorted and snorted, and pawed the ground, like bulls will do; but he never tried to jump that fence again.

I never have heard a dog laugh. My dog, Bert, would smile a lot with his tongue hanging out, but I never heard him laugh. He probably never heard a funny joke or saw anything he thought was funny enough to laugh about.

I have never heard a dog talk either; but the Airport Manager of the Greenville, Downtown Airport in the '70's said his poodle dog could talk. One day he forgot to feed the dog. When his wife got home, the poodle told her all about her absent minded, lazy husband. He said he thought the dog would never shut up. It just went on and on telling on him.

I know another dog that could talk, also, (it was a Chihuahua. The dog was owned by a lady that talked all the time, and the dog was just like her. It yelped all the time (she called it 'Talk", but to me it did not sound like talk. It was just yep – yep – yep.)

The lady would take it for a ride in her car and the dog would hang halfway out the window and speak to everybody it saw.

Maybe this lady could understand what her dog was saying – I couldn't; but she would talk to it all the time and the dog would answer her – like they were carrying on a conversation.

I think that it would probably be easier to make a dog laugh than it would be to make some people laugh that I know. You probably know some, too, like that – those whose mouths are turned down at the edges and those whose noses are turned up (like they constantly smell something bad). (Maybe they do – like their upper lip)

You see a few college professors like that – the more degrees they get, the more they seem to stick their noses up. (Not all of 'em. Just a few of'em.)

I had one like that at Clemson. His nose was turned up like he smelled rotten eggs, and he was grumpy. (Like the old grump in children books that would creep up on little children and scare them half to death.)

I don't believe you could have made that College professor laugh even if you tickled his "funny bone".

But, if old Bert could smile (and he did a lot), and if the Poodle and Chihuahua could talk (as their owners said they did), then, I think it would be reasonable to say: "The little dog laughed when the cow jumped over the Moonie". That would be funny! That might even make that college professor laugh! Don't you think??

TWO LOVE BIRDS

Love is blind. Love is not puffed up. Love is long-suffering...Soul mates. Husband love your wife. That's just some phrases that you have heard, I'm sure, and I have heard...But we are probably all guilty of taking love too lightly.

The atomic bomb is powerful but love could conquer it. If we loved our neighbors as ourselves, the atomic bomb would have absolutely no value. It would be helpless in the face of brotherly love!

I remember making fun of two young people (husband and wife) in love. Look at those silly lovebirds! Hugging one another; whispering sweet nothings to one another; smiling at one another; flashing their eyes at one another; waving at one another. They are silly lovebirds, I thought.

But later in life, I changed my tune. I stood in envy of two old lovebirds this time. They had been married for at least fifty years (his name was Amos. by the way). I came to their house to buy something that they had for sale. But it was hard for me to get their attention to answer some questions that I had for they were all wrapped up in their attention for one another.

While I was looking at the things that they had for sale, I eaves dropped just a bit on the small talk going on between them. Lovebirds, that's what they were. Soul mates, that's what they were. Love is forever. Love is not puffed up. Love is long-suffering. That's what they were, and I envied them. For, frankly, I had missed the mark. I had never experienced a relationship like that.

I knew of another old couple that had been married for a long – long time – like seventy years.

They were old in years and neither was able to take care of all the needs of the other; so they went to a nursing home.

There they had their private room and they were still together.

The old man had a stroke and he couldn't talk; but his wife would talk to him anyway, and she would bath him (the best she could), and feed him (a spoonful now and then). Then one day, after she had bathed him and put clean pajamas on him, and after she had combed his hair he began to mumble something. Then he collapsed in his chair and died.

That night the angels came for her also.

They had spent most of their lives on this earth together and they went out into eternity together – love is forever!

Husband love your wife! Wife love your husbands! Raise your children in an atmosphere of love. Young people love one another, and be sure you are in love before you marry. Then keep that vow forever – even on into eternity for love is forever.

But do you know, there are some people in this world that cannot love. They have never experienced love. Their lives revolve around only their own selfish interests. How pitiful! How sad! Have you known anyone like that? I have met one or two.

I promise you that I will never, ever again, make fun of two lovebirds. Love is the most important force on earth. Without it we are nothing. Without love, we are worth about as much as that tinkling tin can that I kicked on when I was a boy!

COW BARN

Back in the '20's and '30's, the depression days, people had to scrimp
to make ends meet (that's another way of saying they had to pinch
pennies to stay alive).

Most families in those days had a cow, some chickens, and a pig or
two. We kept our cow in a pasture, which was provided by the mill
company for its employees. It seemed that most of the mill company
workers did the same thing. There must have been fifty or more cows
in that pasture of about seventy acres. Consequently, there wasn't
much grass. Everybody had to feed their own cows.

Come milking time, which was early in the morning and late in the
evening, my brothers, John and "Dub", had to go milk our cow. We
fed our cow cottonseed hulls with a hand full of cottonseed meal
thrown in. Our cow liked that.

Cows have a butting order. The cow that butts the hardest rules the cow barn. The cow barn in this case was long (must have been 150 feet) with stalls and feed rooms on each side. Many of the cows in that barn could butt harder than our cow, and they would run our cow away from her feed. Therefore, John and "Dub" had to stay around after they had finished milking until the cow had finished eating (else she wouldn't give much milk).

The cow pasture was used for a lot of other activities besides providing a place for cows. For instance, it was used for a golf course.

Golf courses back then were not nearly as fancy and pretty, with manicured greens, like you see golf courses today. A cow pasture was good enough back then (even with all the "booby traps", "cow piles", "moo cows", etc.).

The golf courses might not have been fancy, but the golfers sure were (only the rich class played golf back then – and they were fancy).

They wore gaudy knickers with knee high socks; white and black winged-tip shoes, with round cleats; white shirts with black poky dots, and a cap made of the same material as their gaudy knickers. (The golfers were a sight for sore eyes.) And I saw them dressed like that playing golf in our mill company's cow pasture. (All I can say is "mercy me".)

Golf has come a long ways since that day. Just about every young man (younger than me) has played the game. (I played one game with my office buddies and I got the "booby prize" – that means I shot the worse score of any. They gave me five dollars for a golf lesson by a pro. I spent the five dollars and put away my clubs. I never took the lesson and I never played golf again). Well, I didn't have the talent for golf. My talent is bragging about my birdhouses.

The cow pasture was used for other activities for us mill village boys. It was our favorite playground. We played baseball down there. Boys from our side of the mill played a team from the other side of the mill. We would gather down there, in the spring, to fly kites. We would have competitions to see who could fly his kite the farthest. Sometimes, we would fly those kites out of sight.

We used the feed rooms to play in when it was raining. We would often build bonfires outside the barn at night and sit around it and tell ghost stories. They got pretty scary and I was afraid that "boogers" would get me on the way home. One old neighborhood man delighted in scaring us. He would lay in wait for us at night and would chase us and said he was going to pull our tongues out with some pliers.

Even though we were poor and times were hard, those were the good old days. That was before big government began telling us what to do and what we could not do. (You know, like stop praying in school, EPA, ACLU, seatbelt laws, and that kind of stuff). I'm afraid the good old days are gone forever; but I can still reminisce, can't I? They can't take away my memories.

BIG DIFFERENCE

There used to be a big difference between little boys and little girls, but you can't always tell the difference today.

Little girls used to dress up in pretty pink dresses, with white patent leather shoes, and each pigtail, hanging down to their shoulders, had a big bow tied at the ends. They smelled good, too, when their mamas dabbed a little dab of perfume behind each ear. They liked that. It made them feel grownup like mama. They had their finger nails painted like mama and they pretended to be mamas - playing house, cooking, sweeping, and rocking and nursing their doll babies.

Little boys were different. They didn't like to get dressed up. They thought it was sissy. They liked to get dirty. They liked to jump in mud puddles and splash water on little girls. They were fascinated with tadpoles, katydids, lizards, and things like that. They would tie strings around June bugs legs and watch them fly in circles. They liked to pull jokes on little girls, especially if they liked them, by putting bugs down their dresses or something like that.

Things are different now. I think it started in Hollywood during World War II. Women went to factories and started doing men's work like riveting, welding and stuff. Hollywood made a movie about it named "Rosie O'Grady" or something similar. Women started wearing pants and shirts and started to look like men. Men started to wear long hair, earrings, and women's stuff and started to look like women. Today, it's sometimes hard to tell the difference.

Women drive dump trucks and work on construction. Men have become airline flight attendants. Women barbers cut men's hair and men barbers style women's hair. Women pilots fly jet fighter aircraft. Men dress up like women and play women's roles in movies. Men stay at home and do the cooking, and washing, and ironing, and raising kids, while their wives go to work and bring in the vittles.

Colleges and universities have opened dormitories to both sexes – male and female rooming together. And, the list goes on and on. WHAT A REVOLTING DEVELOPMENT the world has gotten to be.

No wonder we have so many confused young people today. No wonder we have so many boys and girls and men and women living together without being married. No wonder the morals of this nation have decayed and gotten rotten and stinks to "high heaven". No wonder little babies are being aborted and killed and not given a chance to be born and live, and have life! (Mercy – mercy me! What is this world coming to?)

Life was tough back in the old days; but I know one thing that America possessed that we don't possess today –"Love of God and respect of fellow men." Movies, today, and television make a mockery of God. Four letter words, were not used in the old days – period! Not by spectators at ballgames; not by daddies to their children; not on the streets; and definitely not in movies.

People had respect for God and they had respect for their fellow citizens.

Amos Moses Terry

I wish it was like the old days, don't you, when women were women and men were men and when little girls were made out of sugar and spice and everything nice and little boys were made out of rusty nails and puppy dogs tails – "A Big Difference". I would like that wouldn't you?

OBEY

Obey or else. That was my Mama's orders, (and that's God's orders too). Actually I remember my Mama whipping me only one time. I didn't obey. I gave her some sass. She let me have it with a sapling from a peach tree. She grabbed me by my overalls strap and I couldn't escape. (Maybe that's the reason I remember only one whipping - I usually escaped; but not that time.) She tore me up. She tried to make me say "I'm sorry" but I was stubborn. I wouldn't say it. I wish I could tell her now that "I'm sorry", but it's too late. She's done left to be with the Lord.

I never did get a whipping from my Daddy. Maybe it was because I was scared of him. When he said something, he meant it and I knew he meant it. He was not going to say it twice.

I never got a whipping in school either. I went to school when they still believed in disciplining with a hickory stick. Only our principal used a belt. Some boys got it quite often. One boy got it just about every week. He was contrary and wouldn't obey the rules and sassed the teachers a lot and off to the office he would go. You could hear the slaps of the belt and the yells of pain clear down the hall. (The principal made him pull his breeches down - just in case he had put some padding in his breeches).

Some people are stubborn- like that boy in school. If somebody tells us not to do something, we will be "hell bent" on doing just that.

It's human nature, I guess, to do the opposite from what you are directed to do - like Adam and Eve – God told them not to eat that apple (I guess it was an apple, or it might have been a pear for all I know). Anyway, they ate whatever it was that God told them not to eat, and look what a mess they got the human race into.

It's a "dog eat dog" world – that's what it is!

But old Noah wasn't like that. When God told him to build that Ark, he obeyed. Even though it took him a hundred and twenty years, he stuck with it and built that Ark!!!
Now, that's commitment, don't you think? That's obedience!!

If God tells most people to do something today, it just goes in one ear and out the other. They act like they don't hear Him; or if they do hear Him, they are too busy doing their own thing to obey (just like the population was in Noah's Day).

Jesus said for us to watch and wait and be ready for He's coming back. Are People listening?? Are people obeying??? Shucks no!!!

But I tell you something: "if you belong to God, if you are one of His chosen people, and you don't obey, He's going to whip you". (The whippings that God will give you will be far greater than the whippings that boy got in school!)

. The biggest whipping I ever got was from God. His whippings hurt the most. He didn't use a peach tree sapling or belt. He used a hot iron. He used it to burn a hole in my heart when I didn't obey (which was quite often - I was like that boy in school).

God says something one time and He means it. He's not going to change. I didn't learn this until after many whippings. After each whipping, my heart would hurt so bad. The reason it hurt was because I knew I had betrayed the one who loved me most.

I don't want any more of God's whippings. I have apologized to Him and told Him "I'm sorry", and do you know what? He has forgiven me of all my trespasses. He's a forgiving God like that.

TWEETY

I designed Tweety and painted her in the manner I think God designs birds and fish, and all things in nature and paints them and then He gives them life. But, alas, I cannot give Tweety life. All Tweety can do is sit there with her big wooden head, and with her wooden eyes, and stare at me with a blank look without seeing me. She can't tweet, even though her name is Tweety.

I wish I could breathe the breath of life into her the way God does His creations. Then, she could chirp and sing and fly like all living birds can do.

I have often thought, maybe when I get to Heaven that God will teach me how to design things and then give them life. Wouldn't you like that? Maybe God will teach both of us how to do it. Wouldn't that be wonderful?

Another thing, have you ever wished you could fly? You know, like birds fly? I have many times and I have dreamed that I could. (Have you ever dreamed you could fly)?
What a good feeling it is to dream you can fly like a bird.

When I have dreams like that, it seems that I'm always in a dangerous predicament. I just push myself off the ground and start pushing the air with my arms (like I push the water when I'm swimming) and I just fly up – up and away. I soar like an eagle and people on the ground gawk at me, and stand in awe of me, and ask each other; "how does he do that?"

Do dreams have meanings? I'm sure they do. Most interpreters of dreams would probably say that I'm insecure and am trying to escape something that keeps me bound and "hog tied". But my interpretation would be: "I sure wish I could fly!"

I just feel that it would be wonderful and marvelous to be able to fly all around Iva and out over the beautiful lakes and mountains, above clouds, and look down on all the streams and meadows and flowers – all nature that God has made. (Don't you think that would be wonderful??)

God made this world and all the things in it and then He made man. That means He made all things in this world for man – for you and for me!! He wants us to enjoy His creations.

I would enjoy them a whole lot more if I could fly – and do you know what? I believe someday that I will be able to do just that!!

I have flown a lot already – in airplanes. I have flown around the world five times. (East to West and I have almost flown around the world once from North to South. God has been good to this "ole – country" boy), and I enjoyed the scenery – the Grand Canyon – the ice bergs of Greenland – the mountains of Colorado and the Alps – the barren deserts of Saudi Arabia, etc., etc.; but flying in an airplane would not be nearly the experience as being able to fly like a bird. Now would it?

The sweetest song I believe that I have ever heard was sung by my little granddaughter, Maggie K, and two little colored boys when they graduated from Mrs. Smith's Kindergarten Class in Zebulon, Georgia. They sang; "I Believe I Can Fly."

Maggie K, honey, hang in there for the day is coming when you will fly, and I will fly, and all God's "chillun" will fly. Jesus said that He is coming back and those children of His who are alive will meet Him in the air.

That means we will fly, doesn't it. See there, I told you!

THE FEEDING TROUGH

Pigs like troughs for their slop and I'm sure birds will like them for their birdseed. Pigs that root others out of the way and get to the low end of the trough get the most slop. Take it from me for I'm an expert when it comes to slopping hogs. That was my chore from the time I was about eight until I was about eighteen and finished high school and joined the Army. (Some kids will do anything to get out of doing chores, won't they?).

City boys don't know what they are missing; but I wouldn't trade my experiences for anything. In my opinion, urban boys miss out on a lot of things.

Most of them have never climbed a tree, never stole a watermelon, never built a wash hole out of guano sacks packed with sand, and never went skinny dipping; and have never seen two pigs mate. In short, urban boys just don't have as much fun as country boys!

Let's get back to the fact that a pig that gets to the low end of the trough will get fatter and bigger and more ornery than the others. We had two pigs- a girl pig and a boy pig. The girl pig was the most "piggish" – that is, she would root the boy pig out of the way and get to the low end of the trough; consequently, she got big and fat and the boy pig got puny and skinny (like some runts you see married to bit fat women).

Of course, now, if Paw had castrated the boy pig when it was just a piglet, it might have quit being a gentleman and would have gotten his share of the slop. Then, maybe he wouldn't have been such a runt. But Paw didn't do it. Instead, when the pigs got big enough to understand creation, Paw separated them. He put the boy pig in a separate pen.

The pigs weren't the only ones around our farm that had gotten big enough to understand creation. We country boys understood it, too. It takes city boys a lot longer to learn about the birds and bees. Country boys learn about it when they are just wee-wee little boys from watching all the animals. City boys don't learn about it until they start driving cars. Then they go crazy and make pigs out of themselves.

I was thirteen when my older brother "Dub", and some other boys (I was with them but I had nothing to do with it, I promise!) took some planks out between the sow's pen and boar's pen and let nature take its course.

I will just put it bluntly: "that little boar got even with that big fat sow in a hurry for all the time she rooted him out of the way". I never laughed so much in my life. I rolled and laughed until my belly hurt! That was funny. See, didn't I tell you that country boys have a whole lot more fun than city boys?

Paw never did know about the pigs' romance until the sow was about to have pigs. (Well, he never did ask and I wasn't about to rat on my brothers), if I had, my brothers could have ratted on me about some things, like the time I stole some of Paw's Brown Mule Chewing Tobacco. Hey, don't you rat on me neither for I have quit that nasty habit long, long ago.

But, I'll tell you something: "Dub" and those other boys did Paw a favor by mating those pigs". The sow had six piglets, and we raised all six. We grew a lot of corn and sugar cane and milkweeds (the pigs loved milkweeds. I know for I had to cut those weeds and carry them by the armloads to feed the pigs).

The pigs grew to be big and fat and sassy hogs. When winter came we, slaughtered them, sugar cured the meat, and put the meat in flour sacks, and hung it in the smoke house. (The meat sure was good with Mama's biscuits and homemade molasses).

SIDEWALK CAFE

I don't know why America doesn't have more Sidewalk Cafes. (You know the kind with big colorful umbrellas at tables and with peppermint candy striped awnings). We have a few in the big cities like New York, Miami, San Diego, Atlanta, etc.; but they are nothing like those you see in Europe – especially in France and Italy. I guess Sidewalk Cafes must have originated in France. They are romantic like that.

I enjoy going to them just to watch the traffic. You know the Romeos and Juliets.

If you keep your eyes and ears open you can learn all kinds of stuff at European Sidewalk Cafes -- and you don't even have to know the language. They will charm you with body language.

If you watch and listen you can learn how to treat a lady with real gentlemanly manners and with, oo-la-la, and flattery.

The aroma of the spicy foods is also enticing (I guess that's why they put the cafes on the sidewalks; so that passers by can better smell the irresistible aromas),

All kinds of birds flock to Sidewalk Cafes—some in evening gowns hanging on the arms of guys in tuxedos; some with almost nothing on and with their belly buttons shining; some with funny hairdos and elaborate make-ups. Every now and then, you may see a beautiful pink Flamingo with a real live Turkey; (I never could understand females anyway) or you might see a Duck on the wing of a Penguin to come waddling by.

I think America is missing a lots by not having Sidewalk Cafes".

Burger Kings, McDonalds, Hardees, Popeye's, etc.- eateries that you find in every town of America (even the small town of Iva has two such places) – are not nearly as intimate and picturesque as "Sidewalk Cafes". And the food is not nearly as good in our fast food places as it is in "Sidewalk Cafes".

I think probably the reason food tastes better in "Sidewalk Cafes" than it does in our "hemmed-in" places is because of the atmosphere (and I'm not talking about the temperature or weather conditions either).

I'm talking about the atmosphere of friendliness; the atmosphere of openness; the atmosphere of "chit-chat" between patrons. (All our fast food places seem to want to get you in and get you out – fast).

"Sidewalk Cafes" don't mind if you linger and stay awhile after you have finished eating. (In fact, some of them even serenade you with violin and according music.) That's like, "a little bit of sugar makes the medicine go down".

A little bit of violin and according music makes the food taste "delicious". (Even if it's nothing but fish and chips – a favorite of "Sidewalk Cafes" in "Jolly Old England").

Sidewalk Cafes are real fascinating to me. Are they to you, also???

THE MEETING PLACE

Pigeons and sparrows have a meeting place. They meet every day about sundown in the bell tower of the Iva First Baptist Church. I know they meet there because they drop things all over the pretty green carpet going up the steps.

Some crows had a meeting place in my brother, Alvin's, cornfield, until he built a scarecrow, that looked like him (he may not agree with that) and mounted it on wheels so that he could move it around to different places in the cornfield.

Some cats had a meeting place just below my bedroom window. They seemed to like that place for they met there several times during the week, until I had all I could take of their tomcatting around. One night, when they were having a meeting, I got my pistol out of its secret hiding place and very, very quietly crept over to the window and slowly raised the window, took careful aim above their heads, and then, BANG!!! The cats scattered in different directions. I hated to break up a party (I like parties), but there is a time and a place for everything.

People, like pigeons, and crows, and cats have meeting places. Some meet at ballgames and sporting events. Some meet in downtown lounges and disco joints. Others have secret places, but the best meeting place of all, in my opinion, is in a little white country church, where country folks go, folks who make their living by tilling the soil, who live close to the earth and to nature, and who live close to God.

You see such churches in mountain villages and in Southern small towns.

A friend of mine told me that he once spoke at a small country church like that in the mountains of Georgia. After the service, he was invited to go home with an older couple and have lunch with them.

They drove several miles along a narrow winding, gravel mountain road until they reached their destination – a weather beaten, unpainted, house on the side of a mountain, but it was clean and spick and span on the inside (and, had a wood burning, cook stove in the kitchen),

For lunch, the mountain lady put a gallon of buttermilk on the table and took a big pone of cornbread out of the oven and set it on the table – that was it! That was the lunch that my friend was to share with those mountain country folks that day.

But do you know what? He said that was the best lunch that he remembered eating in a long – long time. For you see, he was a Southern country boy (like me) and he was raised on buttermilk and cornbread (like me). (I wish I had some ice-cold buttermilk right now and a big slice of brown cornbread like the cornbread Mama used to make). Nothing – nothing - nothing tastes as good as the vittles you were raised on!!! (I even like turnip greens, and fatback and fried chicken – course I didn't get much fried chicken back then except on Sundays).

Country folks like country cooking, and country folks have their country churches. I'm still country, and I love "Meeting Places" like that. You can feel the Spirit as soon as you walk in the door!

And I tell you something else about "Meeting Places" like that, it seems like you know everybody there. Nobody is stranger, even though you have not met any of them before in your life.

You know something else? There won't be any strangers in heaven either. The Spirit will make us all feel as one!!

Next time you have a chance, visit a small country church. You will see what I mean.

A BIRD IN THE HAND, ETC, ETC

A bird in the hand is worth two in the bush. That statement had to originate at a place and time when people ate birds (probably in England). The British have a lot of quaint sayings like that. Our forefathers brought them over here and they have been handed down for generations. One of these oldies was: "Sing a song of six pence, pocket full of rye, four and twenty blackbirds baked in a pie; when the pie was opened, the birds began to sing, was not that a dainty dish to set before the king?"

They ate blackbirds. Yuck! We didn't even eat blackbirds, when we were boys cooking down on the creek. But the British did and baked them in a pie. The king ate them, too. That isn't all the British ate that I wouldn't eat. They ate magpies. A magpie is a bird that belongs to the crow family and to the jay family (I thought there was something about a jay bird that I didn't like. Now I know what it is, they are kin to the hoodlum crow.)

You can't blame the British for eating those kinds of things, though. They didn't have as much land as we have to grow things like corn, and beans, and turnip greens, etc.

Even if the British did have enough land to farm, they wouldn't have been able to see how with the smog and fog which hovers over the Isles nine months out of the year.
Besides, it's not good to plow when the ground is wet. It makes the soil lumpy and cloddy and unproductive. The soil in Britton is always wet. They never have a hot day to dry the soil out like we do in the good old Southern part of the USA.

Eating habits are different the entire world over. Chinese, they tell me, eat grub worms, and chickens that have been buried for a long time, and bird's nests. (And they make you take your shoes off).

They tell me that the Arabs like goat meat and they drink gallons of goat milk and camel's milk. I can't criticize their drinking goat milk though. I drank some onetime.
I had stomach problems and a friend of mine, who owned some milk goats, told me to drink some goat milk. (I didn't know if he was lying

and just trying to sell some goat milk or if he was telling me the truth.) I felt so bad and I was in such misery that I decided to try the goat milk. At first, I had to force myself to drink it, but after a few days it didn't taste so bad (it was much sweeter than cow's milk), and sure 'nough, the goat milk cured my stomach problem.

The Arabs will eat goats but they will not eat pigs. You know something? "The Arabs and Jews hate each other" – they are half brothers, but, they hate each other; but, there is one thing that the Arabs and Jews have in common – neither will eat pig meat! I'll bet, if the Arabs fully realized that, that they would stop eating goats and start eating pigs – don't you?

In Malaysia, they eat water lizards, and snails, and crawfish mixed together as a soup in one big pot. They set the pot in the middle of the table and everyone gathers around the table with a big spoon and all eat from the same pot (there's a lot of slurping going on for the soup is hot). Yuck! I was over there and witnessed this. I passed on the soup. I ate raw fish instead (that's another dish the Malaysians have). The fish made me very sick.

I think I would prefer blackbirds baked in a pie. As far as I now, blackbirds baked in a pie might be good (you can't criticize something until you have tried it). Who knows, if I ate some of that pie, I might even start saying: "A bird in the hand, etc., etc."

Some other things that I have eaten: squirrel pie (a squirrel is first cousin to a rat), souse meat (which is made from a pig's head), opossum with sweet potatoes, some of that stuff they served on a shingle in the army, goat meat, horse meat, "chitlins", turtle stew. Did I hear you say, "Yuck"? Me too. I couldn't eat that stuff now.

COTTON HOUSE

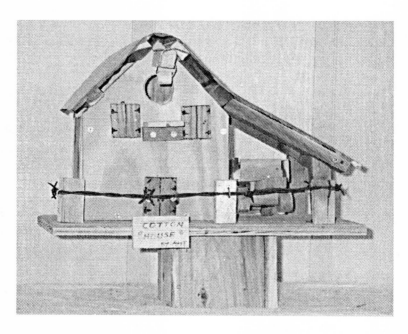

When I was fourteen, we moved from the mill village to a farm. That was a depressing era of my life. Going from a carefree, do as I please youth, to a do as my Papa and my Mama said do farm hand. It was tough for me to get up before the sun and get to the cotton fields and hoe cotton 'till I couldn't see (with some time off for a lunch of beans and cornbread) or to the cornfields and pull corn or fodder; or to the woods and cut wood with an axe (chain saws had not been invented) for cooking and for the fireplace. There were no buddies to hang out with (I sure got lonesome). It was just work, work, work, and work. (Oh my back aches, now, just thinking about it).

One time, my brothers and I were in the fields (my sisters got married young) hoeing cotton on a Saturday morning. It was hot, blistering hot. The ground was rocky, which was rough on my bare feet. It was so hot that I couldn't stand it, so I would put one foot on my leg, to cool it, stood on the other and leaned on my hoe handle. After a bit, I would change the foot that I placed on my leg.

While leaning on my hoe handle like this, I heard the C&WC train whistle toot. As I stood watching it go by, lo and behold one of the boxcar doors was open, and standing there in the door were four buddies of mine from Iva. They were waving like mad. They had hitched a free ride on the freight train to Anderson to see a cowboy movie-probably Tom Mix. I gulped about twice and hung my head to hide the tears trickling down my cheeks, and slowly started chopping cotton again.

Those boys didn't know how lucky they were, I thought; but you know something? After I have got to be a man, I have changed my tune. Hard work never hurt anyone. In fact, hard work is good for boys and girls (I'm not talking about slave labor where children have to labor long hours – making shoes; or rolling cigarettes; or weaving cloth. I'm not promoting factory jobs for children – I'm "agin" that!); but, I don't think it's wrong to assign daily chores for children – such as; slopping hogs, feeding mules, or milking cows. Jobs like that teaches discipline and gets the laziness out.
When kids have been raised like that – to know what work is – they are more apt to stay out of trouble and to make better citizens when they get grown.

Am I wrong? I don't think I am. I don't know the first person that was raised on a Southern farm, that plowed a mule, and chopped cotton, and slopped hogs, and milked cows, that has been in jail for committing a crime; but I know several or I should say "many" that was raised in town, that never hit a "lick of work" in their childhood days.
They did as they pleased and roamed the streets and have been in jail more than once, and have caused society a whole lot of trouble (one of them was in that C&WC Box Car, waving at me, that Saturday morning while I was chopping cotton)!!

Hard work never hurt anyone! <u>All</u> work is honorable – whether it be digging ditches with a pick and shovel; shoveling cow manure out of a barn; drawing water from a well; picking cotton; driving a school bus; or working in a sewer – all work is honorable! Work and chores builds character in children – ask me! I am biased; but that's the way it is!! (PUT THAT IN YOUR PIPE AND SMOKE IT).

Oh, I forgot to tell you about our Cotton House. It was up near the well from which we got our water by using a windless and rope. On Saturdays, after work (we got off a little early on Saturdays), each boy had to draw his own water to take a bath (whether he needed it or not) in a tin tub in the Cotton House.

We also filled that Cotton House to the ceiling with cotton during cotton-picking time. (Oh my back is starting to hurt. So I better quit talking about it).

FRENCH BIRD CHALET

I have been to France only one time. That was when I was a G.I. duringWorld War II. I remember we stopped for a few weeks in Pont a' Mousson. I was a Corporal Telephone Linesman with the 8th Armored Division. We stayed in a barn and slept on piles of hay (that was a pretty good bed compared to some I had to sleep on).

I only know one sentence of French: "Ven a vou aveck moi" or something like that. A buddy of mine from Maine taught me that. He told me to say that when I saw a pretty girl.

When we were riding in a convoy (I in a half-track) through the narrow streets of France, chasing Germans, (that was when we had them on the run), I tried that sentence out on some pretty mademoiselles that were standing in doorways watching us go by. To my disappointment, every one of them shook their heads no. It means, "Will you go with me".

We also stayed a few weeks in a French Monastery, with Monks and Nuns. They were some of the nicest people that I have ever met in my life. The Nuns even took our dirty, filthy GI fatigues and washed and ironed them for us. And they always had a smile on their faces. That told me they had peace in their hearts. Do you know something? I'm Baptist (Southern Baptist) but, I'm convinced that I'm going to see Monks and Nuns and Priests and just plain "everyday" Catholic folks (like my first wife's Mother from Austria) in Heaven. That's going to be quite a reunion. Don't you think that would be a happy time for me to meet those young nuns that washed my clothes while I was a GI Soldier in France: Oh Happy Day!!

Like I said, we stayed in that Monastery for a few weeks, and then British soldiers came and took our places. That was an experience for me, also. We stayed a week or so after the British arrived. We ate together, played cards and games together and got acquainted. The British seem more reserved than we are, but they are not bad "blokes" after you break the ice and get to know them.

I never did really get acquainted with any French Mademoiselles, but one of my buddies did (Gagnon, the GI from Maine that could speak French). One night Gagnon and I went to a French café (he was my interpreter). We sat in a booth (much like a booth in American cafes). Suddenly Gagnon got up and left. I was alone in a French café! But, it wasn't long before he came back – with two Mademoiselles, and they were pretty; but neither could speak a word of English and I couldn't speak French. Gagnon had to talk for both of us (all I could do was sit there and make "goo-goo" eyes at the girls). I don't know what Gagnon was telling them; but it must have been a pretty good line for they both kept looking at me and giggling.

Then the world came crushing down on me! A true-blue good-looking, French Casanova came over and started talking sure 'nough French and he swept those girls off their feet! He flat took them away, and left Gagnon and me holding the bag! That's the nearest I ever came to getting acquainted with a real live, good-looking French Mademoiselle! AIN'T THAT A CRYING SHAME!

I did enjoy seeing many beautiful French chalets in the Alps on the Italian border; however, I must admit that I don't remember what the French birds looked like. I imagine they would look similar to the Mademoiselles. Maybe like the bird I have depicted here (notice the lips, the eyes and the curl).

I'll bet I know something you don't know. All Frenchmen are not lovers (like that Casanova that night). Three out of ten are farmers. What do they grow? Flowers, of course, that are used to make fine perfumes.

WREN HI

There is something that always puzzled me: "Why do little men seem to always have a big, fat wife? Is it because they need someone bigger than themselves to sass around? Little runts are sassy.

I knew a runt once who was my boss and he was sassy. He would square his chin and poke it out at me, like he was inviting me to hit it (The Lord knows there were many times that I wanted to do just that, but I couldn't afford to because he was my boss). He had more ego than Nero, the insane Roman Emperor. He later fired me. I think it was probably because he wanted me to bow down and kiss the diamond ring on his little finger, but he knew I wouldn't do that, so he fired me.

.

Most little runts are sassy.

The little humming bird is sassy. My wife has a humming bird feeder outside our kitchen window. A tiny humming bird, about the size of your little finger, with a red ring around its neck, is the sassiest thing you have seen. Even though it has its belly full, it will sit on a limb and keep watch over that feeder. If other humming birds try to use the feeder, the ringed neck bird will swoop down and chase them away.

The Wren is sassy like that, too. I have several families of them around here. One built a nest in my toolbox. They seem to think this house belongs to them. Every time I come around, they start fussing at me, flicking their tails, jumping from here to there, and chirping wildly. They get all excited.

They build nests all over the place. Anywhere they find a hole big enough to crawl into, they will build a nest. I don't know if they will like apartment living or not. Since they are so sociable, it seems that they would. That's the reason I built Wren Hi. (Another reason is because there is a high school in Powdersville named Wren High School. I guess they must have a lot of wren birds up there, also.)

Wren High in Powdersville is a big school – Class 4A, I think. Crescent High, between the little town of Starr and Iva, is a small school – Class 2A. (That means that Crescent doesn't have nearly the number of students as Wren High). Yet, Crescent beats the "fool" out of Wren every year in girls fast-pitch softball.

Crescent beats the "fool" out of most teams in girls fast-pitch softball – not only Wren, but, other big schools like: Mauldin, Greenwood, Hanna High in Anderson, and others.

Crescent has won more State Championships (seventeen I think) in Class 2A softball than any other school in the world. (Well, at least more than any other school in the USA.) Crescent Coach, Gary Adams, was named National Coach of the year for 2A schools. That's a big honor, don't you think?

The reason Crescent wins so many softball games is because the players have been taught how to hit, bunt, steal, and slide. (Gary

Adams has also coached and trained his girl softball pitchers to throw that ball ninety miles an hour – well you can't hit it if you can't see it.)

Crescent is a small school, yet it is so "frisky" and "peppy" like the little Carolina Wren. I think the name "Wren High" would have been more fitting for the Starr-Iva School than it is for that big school in Powdersville.

Yes, little Wren birds are "frisky" and "peppy". I like them. I think they are so cute. I believe they like me, too, for they fly up to my window and sit there on the back of a chair on the porch chirping at me. They are really domesticated birds - more so than most birds.

Make some Wrens happy. Build them a birdhouse like Wren High and hang it on your back porch. They might like you, too, if you will do that for them.

"OUR GANG"

"Our Gang" was a bunch of boys on black and white television before color was invented. I wish I could remember their names, but for the life of me I can't. I think the gang consisted of five or six boys. One of them was a little colored boy and I think his name was "Buckwheat" – another was "Alfalfa". Is that right? Are you that old? Maybe you can remember.

Anyway, they reminded me of my boyhood days and some of the boys in my neighborhood that were always getting into mischief.

Our Gang (the boys in my group that used to go fishing, squirrel hunting, etc.) consisted of: "Ank" (that's me) "Dub" (that's my brother); "Kirt" (that's short for Curtis), "Peanut" (his real name was Paul), and "Bo" (his real name was Otis). That was our gang. We were not gangsters. We would just play "hooky" from school sometimes and go roaming in the woods, climbing trees, fishing, "skinny dipping", etc. etc.

At first, I sure did miss our gang after we moved from the Mill Village to the country and started raising cotton. (I don't want to get on that subject "cotton" again.)

But I tell you something; it wasn't all that long that I stopped missing those buddies from the Mill Village. You are so busy in the country from sun up to sun down that you don't have time to think about the past. Besides, I met new buddies.

We had some black American buddies. They moved into a tenant house on the farm. (They didn't help us farm. They just rented the house and did their own thing - their mother and sister worked in town); but we became close friends. We would go rabbit hunting together, fishing, and swimming – things that I had done with my buddies in Iva.

We would have fun. I remember my brother, John, and the biggest of the black neighbors, named "Marvin", meeting out at the Indian graveyard (that's what we called a grave plot with stones for grave markers located at the edge of our yard). The purpose of the meeting between John and Marvin was to have a boxing match – with bare knuckles!! They were not mad at each other. They just wanted to see which one could whip the other. Now, John was younger and smaller than I was and I had no trouble whipping him. But, I didn't feel that I was big enough and strong enough and tough enough to take on that big robust, muscular, Marvin!
But, John did! Several times! And stood his ground too. Bop! Bop! Bop! Up side the head they would exchange blows!! I couldn't believe my eyes! .

There were other fun times. I remember one time that we went down to a big creek together. It had been raining, and the creek was out of its banks. The neighbor's little boy, named Eddie, about eight or nine years old, said, "watch me – watch me" and he dashed into the creek – the mighty waters carried him down the creek. His little black head would come up every once in a while. I realized the boy would drown, so I went in and pulled him out. Eddie became my friend from then on.

We had it rough, but our neighbors had it rougher. We did have a cow and plenty of milk. We had chickens, and we got enough eggs to have eggs for breakfast every morning. And, we had hogs and ham and sausage, etc.; our neighbors had none of these. Many times they borrowed corn meal from us, and all they had to eat was corn bread or cornmeal mush.

The black neighbors were our buddies; but we did not form a gang like me and my Iva buddies. As a matter of fact, the only gangs that I was closely associated with in the country were gangs of chickens, goats, pigs, etc. etc. like you see depicted in my birdhouse with the name "Our Gang"

FIELD LARK

When I was a little boy, playing out in a field with my brothers, I noticed a bird that seemed to have a broken wing. It would kick and put one wing on the ground, and flutter. I tried to catch it, to see what was wrong with it; but it seemed to always keep just out my reach. I had chased it, oh, maybe about a hundred feet, when suddenly it took off and flew away. What was wrong with that crazy bird?? It wasn't hurt!! It was just playing a stupid game with me; but I was the one who was stupid – not the bird.

Later, when I told my Mama about the incident (she was a country woman and knew about all birds and wild things), she said the bird was playing tricks on me. She said the bird had a nest nearby and she didn't want me to bother it. That's the reason she played the "old broken wing" trick to lead me away from her nest.

That bird was a Field Lark, but I learned later that Quail and maybe other birds play the same trick. How do they know to do that?? Do you know?? Are birds smarter that we think they are?? (That one was smarter than me).

Next time, I won't chase the bird. I will just run over the nest with my tractor and mower. (Ain't I mean?) Well the bird embarrassed me, and I never did get even.

"UFO"

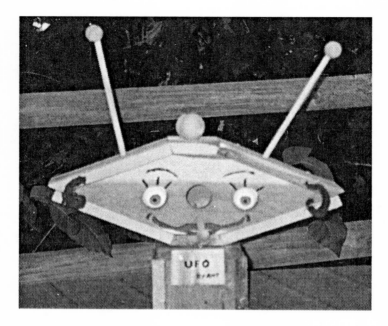

Is it a plane? Is it a bird? Is it Superman? No!! It's an Unidentified Flying Object (UFO).

Have you ever seen one? Me neither! The only UFO's that I have seen was when my brothers threw something at me (watermelon rinds; rotten oranges; eggs; etc.) and I forgot to duck. I often saw those kinds of UFO's when I was a boy!!

But I have never seen a real UFO. You know the kind shaped like a giant saucer, with twinkling lights. One that can move straight up, from side to side or backwards in the twinkling of an eye (say, like a Humming Bird).

I am not saying that these UFO's don't exist. It's just that I have never seen one.

Jimmy Carter saw one and some fishermen out in Pascagoula, Mississippi saw one. So they must exist.

I know Jimmy Carter and those fishermen wouldn't lie, because they are just "good ole Southern boys". Southern boys don't lie. Ask Bill Clinton. He's from Arkansas. Would he lie?? (Ahem, well now, it depends on the definition of what a lie is).

I know that fishermen don't lie. My brother-in-law, Fred McCoy, is a fisherman and he wouldn't lie. He might stretch the truth a little bit, (like the time He said a fish jumped in his boat), but, I don't believe he would straight-out tell a whopper. I ask you! "Would a fisherman lie"??

Chinese and Russians have seen UFO's too. They fly all over Siberia and China. (Why in the world would UFO's want to go to Siberia or China??)

The Chinese and Russians are like George Washington – they have never lied in their lives.

Another thing, UFO's must surely exist; because just about everyone who claims to have seen one tells the same tale: "The UFO came swooping down from out of nowhere and hovered over my car. The lights from it were blinding. It squirted some kind of oil-like substance all over my car and the windshield. The UFO sapped all the energy from my car and my car quit running – the battery was drained DEAD! The UFO then turned sideways and sailed, like a Frisbee, into outer space".

That's the tale they all tell except for that fisherman in Pascagoula, Mississippi. His tale was different: "I was sitting in my bateau at the mouth of the Pascagoula River, fishing for Bluegill Catfish. (I was using chicken guts for bait). I admit, I had drunk a pint or two of "malt liquor" (that's about one hundred proof booze) when a huge something that looked like a giant saucer landed on the river. A great big sliding door opened up on the strange craft, and three small creatures (about the size of a three foot tall midget) came down the gangplank and waded over to my bateau. I remember they were kinda weird – they each had a great big eyeball in the center of their heads;

they had cauliflower ears about the size of a baseball glove; their noses were just two holes in their faces; and they had just a slit (no lips) for their mouths that reached from ear to ear. (I saw them clear as day – they didn't look blurred like things normally look when I've been drinking malt liquor). They zapped me with some kind of ray gun that paralyzed every muscle in my body, except for my brain (I knew everything that was going on). They took me aboard their craft and put me under some kind of x-ray machine – they examined my brain, my bones, and my organs. They put me back in my bateau and they flew away. Oh, by the way, I caught a twenty pound Catfish that day that had one great big eyeball instead of two."

Now, I know that UFO's surely exist for I ain't never heard a fisherman's tale like that! All the fisherman I know tell little bitty tales. None of them could make a tale up like that – not even those from Mississippi (Texas, yes – but not Mississippi)!!

COUNTRY SHACK

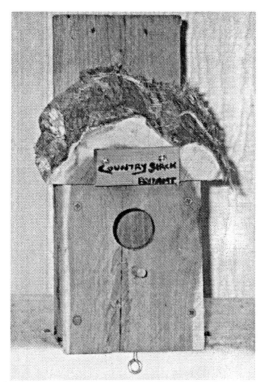

I'm not an evolution enthusiast. That is, I don't subscribe to the big bang theory. I think that theory is a bunch of junk dreamed up by some scientists that have wires crossed in their brains.

I believe that there is a God in control of everything. I also believe that His ways are not our ways and we don't understand His ways.

And another thing, if people did evolve from apes or monkeys, so be it, that was God's way of creation. But at some point and time, God created man in His own image and man became a living soul. Man was created by God with a free will in order that God might have fellowship and companionship with man. Man is capable of becoming the Sons of God and if he becomes God's Son, that means he has an inheritance awaiting him - the inheritance of God's Kingdom. That's what I believe. (No. That's what I know. I know, I know....that Jesus liveth,.....and on the earth.....again will stand). Do you know, too? I hope you said yes. But, if you said no, come see me and we will talk about it

There is no doubt about it. Things are evolving. People today are much smarter than they were sixty-seven years ago (when I was a boy of eight). I know this to be a fact. And people are getting smarter each day (they may get too smart for their breeches one day soon).

I know people are smarter because they don't eat cornbread and buttermilk, and pinto beans for their main meal six days a week like they used to (now they can have fried chicken seven days a week. All they have to do is run down to Kentucky Fried Chicken and buy some).

People are smarter because they don't have to take their families to church in a two-horse wagon with straight chairs in the back for the women folks to sit. (Now each family member drives his own car.)

People are smarter because they don't live in rickety old unpainted country shacks with cracks in the floor and ceiling, and with a fireplace that would burn the legs and hind end off of women folks who stand too close to the fire.

There are a lot of other things that tell me people are smarter today than they were years ago. Women don't have to worry about keeping the seams straight in their nylons, and they don't have to use pieces of rubber inner tubes to keep their hose up – they wear panty hose without seams and with elastic bands at the top. Women and men don't wear hats anymore – they wear caps with logos of their favorite sports team. Children don't have to go barefooted and cut their feet and stub their toes – parents today are making enough money to buy their children shoes. We don't have to sit up close to radios to hear the news and listen to sporting events. We can sit back in our recliner and zap the television with remote controls and flick the channels to a station we like.

Country Shacks are a thing of the past. People today live in brick houses, high-rise apartments, and mansions – ain't that smarter?

And one last thing, people can turn the water on in their houses today and wash their faces. They don't have to wash their faces in a pan and throw the dirty water out the back door like they once did.

BACK YARD FEEDER

Some bird feeders belong in the front yard and some belong in the back yard. You didn't know that did you? But I guess it depends on the layout of your house. You want to place the feeders where you can see the birds feeding. (Ain't I smart?)

My house has bay windows in the kitchen which are on the front part of my house. We spend a lot of time at a table in front of the bay windows. My wife has placed "stick on" humming bird feeders on the bay windows (I call these front yard feeders).

Our driveway comes by the front of the house and goes all the way around the house. Across the driveway from the kitchen, I have placed a large cedar "Early Bird Cafe" feeder mounted on a pole. It looks good. It looks rustic, the way I like it. That's another front yard feeder.

The front yard feeders can be seen from the highway, which is down a hill from my house. I like to use nice feeders and birdhouses in the front yard where "passer bys" might see them. If my front yard feeders were "not so nice", then people passing by might think "sho' nough" country folks live here, and I don't want them to think that.

My back yard feeders don't have to be so nice because only kinfolks and close friends see these feeders. It ain't no need to dress up the back yard just to impress these folks. They know already that "sho' nough" country folks live here, and nice bird feeders won't change their minds.

Another thing, back yard feeders don't have to be all that pretty to attract birds of different feathers – any old bird feeder will do as long as it holds enough bird seed.

As a matter of fact, I have found that back yard feeders made of natural wood and unpainted will attract more birds than fancy looking, painted front yard bird feeders. (What is the purpose of the feeders? Is it to attract birds or to look at?) To attract birds, of course.

And my back yard feeders do attract birds – lots of'em. Red Cardinals, Sparrows, Blue Birds, Wrens, etc. They also attract something else – squirrels.

I put the feeders on a pole, high off the ground and put aluminum around the pole from the ground to the bottom of the feeders – so that squirrels can't climb the pole and get into the feeders – but, they still get in them. They climb out on limbs of shrubbery and jump to the feeders. Squirrels are a nuisance to me and to the birds! (I made them some squirrel feeders (not shown in my book) with a spike to hold an ear of corn; but the squirrels won't eat from their feeders – they are like the birds, they prefer my "Back Yard Feeders".

I'll tell you something else about squirrels, they will get in your house if you aren't careful, and, they will gnaw holes in everything. The way they will get in is similar to the way they get in my "Back Yard Feeder". They will climb a tree that has limbs near the house. They will go out on the limbs and jump to the house. Then, if your house has any wood on the gables, the squirrels will gnaw holes through the wood and get into the house. (They got into a rental house I had like that and I had a time getting rid of them.) I had to cut all the trees near the house and patch the "gnawed out" holes – squirrels are rodents and they can be a nuisance!

MARTIN FAMILY HOUSING

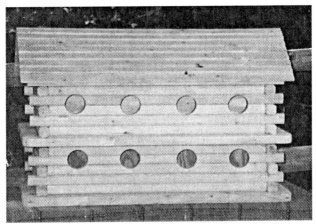

Gene Autry used to sing a song, the first line of which goes something like this: "Give me land, lots of land, underneath the starry skies above...don't fence me in".

Like Gene, I'm a country dude myself. I like lots of room. I don't want to be fenced in.

When you start fencing people in, they lose control (like fenced in animals lose control and have to depend on their masters and have to do as their masters say do).

The Federal Government has fenced in a lot of people; consequently, these people have lost control. Like fenced in animals, they have become totally dependent upon their master, the Federal Government. They expect the government to provide them with shelter, food, and the necessities of life (which the government does).

You can see these shelters, government family housing projects, in every town and city across America. The government dishes out food, in the form of food stamps, to these dependent, fenced in animals (oops, I mean unfortunate people). Other necessities of life, such as; medical assistance, child support, fuel costs, etc., etc., are provided to these caged in folks. And sometimes, in a lot of cases, these folks are healthy, robust, but lazy lay-abouts.

Amos Moses Terry

I don't believe any of them are as poor as I was when I was a country boy living on a farm; but my parents were different. They believed in working and earning our own bread and necessities of life. As poor as we were, my Daddy would not take "hand-outs". It was an insult to him for someone to offer him a" handout".

I realize that sometimes people need a helping hand -- when they have health problems or when they get too old and too feeble to work, and when they are not able to take care of themselves; but (like my daddy was) it aught to be an insult for able bodied, healthy people to take "handouts"! Opportunity abounds for all people, who are able, to earn their own way.

I don't agree with Government's philosophy. I don't believe we are helping individuals by giving them "handouts". I don't believe our Society is becoming better by encouraging lazy people to accept a free ride from hard working citizens who pay taxes for these "handouts".

I'm sure that these folks would be a lot happier, they would feel better about themselves, and the community would treat them better, and they would have more dignity, if the Federal Government would tear down those fences and allow these folks some freedom. (Freedom to work, freedom to go to school and get an education, freedom to get out of the family housing units and own a home of their own, a home that they would be proud of because they have earned it for themselves).

I believe they would be a lot happier, don't you? "Let me straddle...my old saddle....underneath the western skies....don't fence me in".

I think family housing is for the birds-like Martins. Don't you?

MISS BOSSEY

When I was a boy, long, long time ago, People would give names to their cows, mules, goats, horses, etc. I don't think they do that now. There are so many that they just stamp numbers on tags and clamp them to their ears. Names are not often used, especially for cows.

At least that is so with my brother, Alvin. He has about fifty cows and they all have numbers. (It's easier for Him to call the roll that way.) Except for one cow He likes so much that He gave her a name - "Big Red". He's in the beef business and the reason He likes her so much is that she's a big hunk of beef and has beefy calves. (He could have named her "Big Dollar" that would have fit better for that's what she is to Alvin.)

Hey, that reminds; me, did you see where a red heifer was born in Israel? The first red heifer born in Israel in something like 2000 years. They tell me that the daddy of the heifer was black and her mama was white. Israel is saving that heifer to sacrifice on the altar when they

111

get the new temple built. The Arab Moslems want to shoot the heifer. That's what I wanted to do to a cow that would butt our cow and run her away from her food. "Miss Bossy", that's what I called her.

"WHOA NELLIE"

There are three kinds of mules - Jacks, Emma's, and Nellie's. At least, that's what we had on our farm. My brother, "Dub", and I plowed the Jacks; Paw plowed old Emma, and my brother, John, plowed old Nellie.

The only difference between the Jacks and Old Nellie was: "the Jacks were a he, and Old Nellie was a she" Old Emma was a she too, but she was an obedient, humble mule. That's the reason Paw plowed her.

The Jacks and Nellie's were a mess. They were sure 'nough stubborn mules. The Jacks would try to run with the plows and Old Nellie didn't act like she knew what gee and haw meant. (And whoa neither!)

The Jacks would run with something else too, the wagon. One day "Dub" and I went into the woods with the Jacks hooked to a wagon to get a load of firewood. After we got there "Dub" asked me to stand in front of the wagon and hold the reins of the mules while he loaded the

113

wood. As soon as I took the reins, the Jacks started jumping up and down and rearing up like they were fixing to pounce on me with their hooves. I got scared and dropped the reins and dashed for safety. The mules took off with the wagon. They seemed to be going at least fifty miles per hour, and do you

know something? "Dub" outran those mules and jumped on the wagon and started sawing the bits in their mouths with the lines and stopped those "run-away Jack Asses". I stood in amazement, awe, and wonder at my brother! He was some more man!

The jacks would run with something else too – a plow. I never saw such contrary mules in all my life.

I was plowing cotton one day with a jack and he decided to be contrary. He started walking on top of the cotton instead of in the furrow, like all good mules do. I told him to gee and he wouldn't gee! I told him to haw and he wouldn't haw. In fact he wouldn't do anything I told him to do. (I would even try to coach him to get off the cotton by jerking a little bit on the plow lines; but the idiot continued to walk on the cotton.) Finally, I got mad! I gave a big jerk, I mean a big – big jerk on the plow lines and that fool mule took off running and I plowed up a whole row of cotton before I could get him stopped!!

I was glad when Paw took those jack asses (both of 'em) to a sale and traded them for two "work horses". The horses were not all that smart (they only had "Horse Sense") and they didn't know any better than to do what they were told to do. Plowing was a whole lot easier when they were pulling the plow. (They were not nearly as mule-headed as the jack asses.)

But, we still had old Nellie. She was a big, tall, long legged, black mule. She was independent and contrary. If you got too close to her "hind-end", she would kick at you. She always watched you out of the corner of her eyes, and, if she saw a chance to kick at you, she would do it!! (When you hooked her to a plow, you had to be extra, extra

careful. I knew how to handle her, though, and I wasn't scared of her –
if she thought you were scared, she would really get contrary)!

Old Nellie could run too. One day my brother, John, and I were taking
turns plowing with her, breaking ground for a watermelon patch.
After we were finished, John and I had an argument over who was
going to ride the mule home. I was bigger and older, so I jumped on
the mule's back. This made John mad, so he took the plow lines and
gave Old Nellie a big whack on her rump and shouted "Go Nellie
Go", and old Nellie took off. I shouted "Whoa Nellie Whoa", but
remember I told you she didn't know what whoa meant. She got faster
and faster and bounced me off her back. John laughed and hee hawed.
A very embarrassed, silent, Amos Moses followed Old Nellie to the
barn.
#X!!*DDD****XXXX! NELLIE I TOLD YOU TO WHOA!!!!!

"OINK"

I wonder do pigs talk to each other?

I know for sure that Canadian Geese do. A flock of them flew over my house one day and I could hear them jabbering away at each other.

Bantam Roosters talk too. At least they talk to the hens. I have heard them say: "tick-wrong-wrong-wrant" and the hens would get all excited like they knew exactly what the rooster was talking about.

We had an old male guinea that talked to the chicken hens, too. He had been run over by a car and was lame in one leg, but that didn't keep him from talking to the hens. He was very aggressive, like he had just come over from Africa. It was funny to watch him.

Did you know that male guineas would mate with chicken hens? I didn't either, but that one sure did – and we had some half guineas –

half chickens to prove it. They weren't very pretty – in fact, they were ugly; but they tasted all right when Mama fried them good and brown.

Our cow could talk, too. She was a jersey and she used to give a lot of rich – creamy milk; but her milk production fell way off to just a trickle – we didn't get nearly enough milk for all our hard working family.

So, my brothers, John and "Dub", one day, decided to breed her – that might help her milk production they thought. So they took her down to our neighbor's pasture where there was a big red, short horn, beef bull that weighed about two thousand pounds. My brothers opened the gate to the pasture and turned our cow loose. She went running – I mean fast – to that bull and such mooing you have never heard! The bull heard her and he came running too and bellowing – those two animals talked to each other that day!

Later, our cow had the prettiest heifer that you have ever seen. It was big, and fat, and red like her daddy.

One day, a neighbor boy and I thought that calf was so fat and pretty that we would take her to the county fair and show her off and she might win a blue ribbon or something. So my friend borrowed his daddy's pickup with high side bodies and we loaded that calf aboard and started to the Anderson County Fair Grounds with her. We didn't get forty feet 'til that calf jumped over those high side bodies of the truck and escaped and went running to her maw!

Our cow was sure jealous of her calf. If you starting messing with the calf, the cow would come running and mooing, just like she did that day she met that bull! (Oh by the way, our cow did start giving more milk – gallons of it!)

But, pigs? I don't think they can talk -- not even in Pig Latin. When I was a boy, I learned to speak Pig Latin. A lot of other boys did too, and we could carry on a conversation in Pig Latin. We could make fun of other kids who didn't know Pig Latin and they didn't even know what we were talking about. Listen: "ooyea, omeka, ootay, eesay, emay". Translation: "you come to see me", or did you know that already because you talk Pig Latin too?

I'm satisfied pigs don't know Pig Latin, English or any language. All they can say is "oink". Pull their tails and they will say "oink-oink". That's all folks!!!

BROWN THRASHER'S CABIN

Freckles are cute-especially on little girls with auburn colored hair. Especially, if that auburn hair is braided into long pigtails with ribbons at the ends.

I can see her now. Her name was Margaret. I think she liked me a little bit; but I didn't like her. She had freckles, and I didn't think freckles were cute back then like I do now. I thought freckles were for tough boys like me. I had them, too, across my nose and on my cheeks.

Maybe that's the reason I didn't like freckles. When I made some of my buddies mad, which was quite often, they would call me names -- like "Amos and Andy" (I didn't like that) and like "freckled face and snotty nose" (I didn't like that either). When they called me these things, I was ready to fight. (You can tell that I was a scrapper, can't you?)

It's funny how values change over the years. I didn't like cornbread and buttermilk when I was a boy, now I do. I didn't like my name, "Amos" (and I got into a lot of fights because of it) now I'm proud of that name. I think it is distinguished, don't you? You better say yes!.

119

Back when I was a boy, I thought freckled faced little girls were "tom boys" and not very pretty. Now I think they are the cutest things under the sun. They are almost as pretty as a Brown Thrasher. That's an auburn colored bird with freckles.

Brown Thrashers are pretty, and do you know what? A Brown Thrasher's eggs have freckles too – isn't that something?

Can you tell what kind of bird it is by seeing her eggs? I used to be able to do that when I was a boy: for instance, I know that Brown Thrasher's eggs have brown freckles (like the birds that laid them: Blue Bird's eggs are pale blue; a Cat Bird's eggs are pale gray (like the Cat Bird). That's just a few - but I used to be able to identify <u>all</u> birds that live around Iva by looking at their eggs.

Do you know something else? I read where now they are able to produce chicken hens that will lay colored eggs. (Some hens will lay blue eggs; some red; some green; some yellow, etc.) No longer does a mother have to go to the trouble of dying Easter eggs for her children. She can just go down to the super market and buy natural colored eggs. (Don't quote me on this. It's just something I read and sometimes you can't believe everything you read).

I don't know if this new chicken hen will be able to lay multi-colored eggs (you know, like the freckled Brown Thrasher's eggs). I don't believe that man has gotten that smart. There are some things only god can do – like design birds in all different sizes, shapes, and colors and <u>what's so amazing</u> is for the birds to lay eggs that match their colors – I believe that only God can do that!!

Nature is so wonderful. We old folks don't get out and enjoy nature enough like we did when we were young. We sit, too much, in our easy chairs and watch television. If something interesting comes on Discovery Channel, concerning nature and wild life, we might watch that for a while; but, it's not like getting outside, down on the creek, and taking a romp in the woods, like we did when we were youth.

We just don't appreciate and love life like we used to. When I was a youth, I found birds and their habitats enchanting – there was a mystery about them. Do you know what I think that my story is? God's hand is over it all – even the sparrows!!

WOOD PEWEE

Have you ever shot marbles when you were young? I doubt it. You are probably not that old. We shot a lot of marbles when I was a boy (for keeps too), and we wore a lot of holes in the knees of our overalls, too. Sometimes when we had been shooting marbles for a long time, we would rub all the skin off our knuckles.

I was a pretty good marble shooter; but I wasn't the best. A boy that lived on the other side of the cotton mill was the best. He carried his marbles around in a 24- pound self-rising flour sack (that's a middle size flour sack). I think a 48-pound was the biggest. That's the size that was used at our house. We ate a lot of biscuits and butter and molasses and fatback.

We used to have some pretty big marble games with maybe six or seven boys in the game. The better marble shooters used bigger circles. Our circles were usually about 20 feet in diameter. We had rules – no fudging (you had to keep your knuckles flat on the ground) and you could shoot a hand-span away from the ring or your marble.

To start the game, the marbles were placed in a clump in the center (like billiards). Each player contributed – say five marbles or more. Straws (or matches) were drawn to determine who would break the marbles (1stshooter, 2nd, etc.) The game lasted until all the marbles had been shot out of the circle. Each player kept the marbles he was able to shoot out.

We used our best marbles to do the shooting. Sometimes these marbles were bigger than the others. They would thump better and sometimes we used steel balls as our agates. (That's what we called our marbles used to break).

The boy from the other side of the mill used a steel ball and sometimes, when he got to break, we wouldn't even get a shot. He would make a run and shoot every last marble out of the circle before he was through. (That's the reason he carried his marbles in a 24-pound flour sack).

We had some pretty glass marbles. (We also collected and traded marbles). We had some that were not so pretty – some were pitted (from being hit numerous times in a marble game) and others might have a crack or chip missing.

Every once in a while some cheap lad would try to sneak a Pee Wee into a game. (A Pee Wee was forbidden in our games). A Pee Wee was a marble made of clay instead of glass. (That was a "sho 'nough" poor boy's marble).

The clay Pee Wee is not the kind of Pewee that is the subject matter here. The subject that we are talking about here is a Wood Pewee. A Wood Pewee is not even a wood marble. IT'S A BIRD!

As a matter of fact, a Wood Pewee is a tiny bird related to the flycatcher. The reason it is called a Pewee is because when it tweets it goes "pee-ah-wee". If you get up early enough you might hear one tweet for it tweets at daybreak and again in the evening when shadows begin to fall. (It's not like a lot of other birds that tweet all the time ' say like the hoodlum crow and blue jay).

It likes the woods, and thickets and marshes and wetlands – places where bullfrogs and katydids, flies and mosquitoes hang out. ('course it doesn't eat frogs, but it eats flies). I made Wood Peewee's birdhouse so that it would blend in with such an environment. I hope a Wood Peewee will come and build a nest in it!

THIS PHONE IS FOR THE BIRDS

It hasn't been all that long ago, maybe about 50 years, when most towns and cities had patch panel switchboards. Operators sat on stools in front of the switchboards. When someone called another, the call would go to the operator. She would take a cord and plug the ends into holes and connect the two parties together so that they could talk.

Iva had one operator with a switchboard in her home. The switchboard had about one hundred holes. That's how many people living in Iva that had phones. Not many.

My Father-in-law's number was two. I guess he was the second person in Iva to have a phone. Now, everyone has phones. There are phones in every room. There are phones that people carry with them wherever they go. Soon there will be television for phones. People will be able to have an eyeball to eyeball chat.

There used to be phones that you could use to call up catfish (until they outlawed them). They were the old hand crank type. I have used them in the Savannah River,
before they dammed it all up. Some buddies and I used to go telephoning catfish. That was a lot of fun!

The catfish would always answer the phone, even if they were busy eating on the bottom or sleeping under a rock. They would come up to the top of the water to see who was calling. They were so anxious to answer the phone that only their tails would be touching the water.

My Father-in-law used a phone like that one time on a fishing partner when he was bent over getting out of his wet breeches. The partner yelled, jumped sky high, and took off running down through the woods. When he realized what had happened, he came back and said: "You fool, you?"

Antique phones (like the phones used for cat fishing) have a high price today. My wife just bought one. She paid a lot of money for it, too. (Why is it, when things get old and out of date that people will pay lot of money for the old items?) Like I said about that antique telephone that my wife bought, she can't use it. The sounds coming in over the line will be like a bunch of "garble-de-gook" compared to the clear, filtered sounds of new versions of phones -- and another thing, my wife can't walk around all over the house using the antique phone. She will have to stand right there at the phone to do her talking (the mouth piece is part of the phone).

I don't know what good the antique phone is though, except maybe to make a birdhouse out of it. (Well, if people and catfish can have phones, why can't birds)?

But, the "phone like" birdhouses that I have made has money slots. (for dimes and nickels and quarters). Now that was stupid of me, wasn't it? No bird is going to have money to spend to make telephone calls – unless it happens to be a sparrow – now a sparrow might find some money and weave it into her nest, (that is, if the money is folding money – they will only accept folding money. No change).

So there again, I guess it was futile of me to make a phone birdhouse with money slots. No bird is smart enough to take folding money down to the bird feed store and get change, in order that she might make a phone call.

So, I guess this phone that I have made is for the birds in more ways than one!!! (Oh, my, me!).

CAT BIRD INN

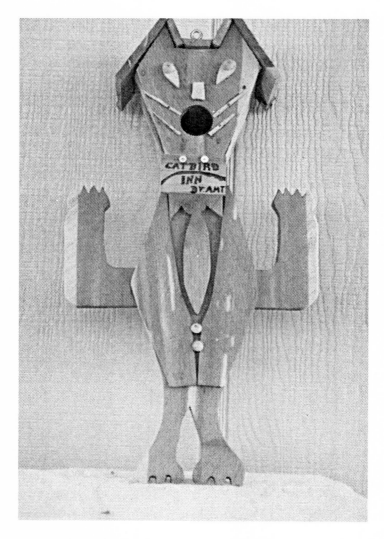

When I was a boy, living on the mill village in Iva, a bunch of us boys, ten to fifteen years old, would get together and hike to the country to find a hole in a creek deep enough to go skinny dipping in to cool off a bit.

I remember one time my brother, "Dub", got his clothes off before I did and jumped into the water. I hollered at him: "Hey, 'Dub', how deep is the water?" He hollered back: "pecker deep". That was deep enough for us boys.

We were outdoors boys. We climbed trees, trapped rabbits, flew kites, swapped bantam chickens, caught tadpoles, looked for baby pigeons on top of Iva Schoolhouse, climbed water tanks, and barely stayed out of trouble.

We often had cookouts. We roasted birds (robins and doves), fried fish (mostly minnows we caught seining in creeks with burlap sacks), fried rabbits, and I remember one time we fried some chitlings down in the mill company's pasture. They tasted pretty good too, something like bacon.

Back then, I could tell you the name of every tree by its leaves, every bird by the color of its eggs, the name of every snake and whether it was poisonous or not. I thought city boys were dumb because they didn't know all those things.

But there was something that always puzzled me: "How did a cat bird get its name?" I guess it was because it sounds a tiny bit like a cat (meow). Or does it? I'm not sure it does.

But I always thought it resembled a Mocking Bird. (It is first cousins to the Mocking bird, but, it is not nearly as mean). Cat Birds live in thickets down on the creek while Mocking Birds nest almost anywhere.

Mocking Birds particularly like my Father-in-law's fig bush. They nest in it every year. And, like I said, they are so mean they will chase every other bird away.

The Mocking Bird likes to sing and it knows a zillion songs. It can sing songs that you have never heard before (like:"caw-caw"; "squak-squak"; "quack-quack"; "yoo-hoo-babe"; "when the roll is called up

129

yonder" (and a lot of other good old Southern numbers). A Mocking Bird can imitate as many and twenty local bird species.

I saw a comedian once that could imitate Richard Nixon – and George Bush (the old man). They made a mask of George Bush and I saw the guy put it on and he talked just like George Bush. It was hilarious!! I laughed 'til my belly ached.

The Mocking Bird is a big imitator, but is a good singer. As far as I know, the Cat Bird, which is the Mocking Bird's first cousin, can only sing one tune, (and the Mocking bird can even copy that tune).

I once knew a guy like that. He would copy everything you said to him. If you said: "I think you are a lowdown, good for nothing, finger licking, scoundrel", he would respond: "You think I'm a lowdown, good for nothing, scoundrel:" I don't care what you said, he would repeat it--but he wouldn't hurt a fly!

That's what a Mocking Bird is – a copycat – but, the Mocking Bird is a fighter. It will fight birds – it will fight cats, and it will fight people. It's like a Pit Bulldog, "born to fight".
Cat Birds are a little like that, but, they better look out for those "Putty Cats"!!! (for "Putty Cats" will catch them and eat them, too). I thought I saw a "Putty Cat"! I know, I know I saw a "Putty Cat", (but it was only a bird house by that name)!

EL SENORITA

"South of the border....down Mexico way...that's where the stars at night....come out to play...and now as I wonder....when life was so gay....south of the border...down Mexico way....Hi..Yi..Yi..Yea...Hi...Yi..Yi..Yea!!!"

That's a verse of a song (or something like it) that I learned when I was a boy, many years ago, and I haven't forgotten it after all these years.

I can close my eyes, and still see the Mexican peon who sang it and drummed it on his old guitar, along with many other Mexican songs. He entertained a bunch of us cotton mill village boys as we gathered around him on Miss Kizzy Well's front porch. (She gave him room and board).

131

I have heard some other Mexican songs, since then, when I went to Tijuana a couple of times, once with some buddies of mine, and again with my wife and daughter.

When I went with my buddies, we heard all kinds of songs, and that's not all, we witnessed some unusual sights, too (by Mexican senoritas on stage).
The words: "when life was so gay" in that verse of the song are true. Life is gay in Mexico. They are a happy-go-lucky people (especially the   dancing   senoritas).
"Cha...Cha...Cha...Clickey...Clickey...Click...Stomp...Stomp...Shake... Shake...Shake". Fascinating. (I wonder what makes them so lively? Probably the hot tamales they eat).

There is something about life "South Of The Border Down Mexico Way" that attracts me. I guess it's because I can identify with those poor Mexican peons.

Most of them live a simple life. That's one thing, I know, that is attractive to me! I like simple people, people who are satisfied with themselves, and who do not try to pretend to be something they are not (what you see is what you are). I found Mexicans and South Americans to be just that.

Another thing that I like about them is their friendliness – they do not hold anything in reserve – they are open, and friendly and happy-go-lucky people. They give of themselves without expecting some great rewards in return. They have got something here that is valuable. I wish I could be more humble and friendly and open like they are. (Neighborliness I guess would be a better word!)

Lastly, they are hard workers. No work is below their dignity. They are willing to crawl under a house, and get dirty, and sweat and do hard labor.

I have been remodeling and old Southern home that is about one hundred years old. I had to crawl under it to do some plumbing and electrical work. I told my son Bill, who lives in California about my crawling under the house and he said: "Dad, that's why we grow Mexicans, to do work like that". That's true and thank God for them – no work is below their dignity. We need more Americans to be like that!!

Life is gay South of the border. I wish life would be so gay here! We live too fast. We live too isolated. We live too "hum-drum".

Another thing I noticed about the people south of the border is their love for family. They love their daddies – they respect their daddies. Their daddies are their heroes (course they love their mamas too) but, I admire their love and respect for their daddies – I wish my children would take a lesson from them. Over here it seems mamas are the most important. South of the border daddies are still head of the family.

"Mexically Rose keep smiling...I'll come back to you...some sunny day". El Senorita keep those pretty red lips smiling and you will keep all those honchos and peons happy

THE CROW'S NEST

Crows are smart birds. They are not nearly as dumb as they pretend to be. A lot of farmers don't like them because they peck holes in their watermelons, pluck up sprouting corn plants, eat the seed and get most of the corn that makes a crop before the farmer can harvest it.

They are smart. They travel in gangs, and they talk to each other. I don't know their language, but I believe "Caw-Caw-Caw" means" it's time to scat"; or it might mean "the old man has a gun. Let's get out of here"; or it could mean, "the last one out is a rotten egg (or a dead duck)"; or something like that.

If you catch young baby crows, you can tame them and teach them to talk.

I have heard (from tales of yore) that if you split their tongues, they can say most anything

I have never heard one with a split tongue talk but I bet it would cuss like a sailor. Crows impress me as being a rowdy type like that.

When they are stealing watermelons, they always post one crow on a nearby fence post. That's the lookout crow. This sentry warns the other crows when someone is coming.

Just like on a ship (before they invented radar) a lookout sailor, with a big long telescope, was posted high up on the main mast in a shelter called a "crows nest". He was the one who shouted (just like a lookout crow) to the crew below" Pirates are coming, let's get out of here".

The lookout sailor had to be the bravest and most alert sailor on the ship. It was a dangerous job being way up there in that Crow's Nest on the main mast! I imagine that he would be the first to go (to die) if the ship encountered pirates. The pirates knew that if they could make that main mast fall that the rest of the crew would be like "setting ducks". So, you can bet that the first thing that the pirates would aim their big cannon ball guns at would be the main mast and that guy up there in the Crow's Nest!

The lookout sailor also had to be an old tar – an old salt - a veteran sailor! - One that had sailed the ocean many times in all kinds of inclement weather – one that when the sea billows rolled, he didn't get seasick. For there would be many times, when he was up there in the Crow's Nest, that storms would surely come. The seas would surely roll and tumble. The Crow's Nest would surely sway, until it seemed that it would touch the waters – but, the old – veteran tar in the Crow's Nest would stay on watch … and would be able to shout out instructions to the crew below in case of dangers!!!

I admire old sailors of yesteryear when sailors were just that – sailors! I admire their captains and navigators and the old tars in the Crow's Nests.

Listen: "I admire old crows, too, especially those that sit on fence posts and serve as lookouts for those that are stealing watermelons, or cantaloupes, or corn"! I think they are smart and brave and I don't care what Southern farmers say!

Old tars and old crows have a lot in common. I guess that's the reason why someone, a long time ago, named the "Look Out Station" on a sailing vessel "The Crow's Nest" (how appropriate). I don't know who it was, but I'll bet he probably was a wise old retired sailor that had settled down on a Southern farm and probably raised watermelons.

OLD TAR'S LIGHTHOUSE

An old tar was a veteran sailor, one who had salt water in his veins instead of blood (for this reason, sometimes, they were called old salts). Old tars, old salts, old sea dogs are one and the same - a veteran sailor.

Their boats were made of wood and not steel like our ships of today. They were powered by muscle power, oars, and with wind power, sails. They had no diesel or atomic powered engines.

They had crude compasses, but navigation was usually accomplished by watching the sunrise and set by day and by knowing the locations of certain stars by night. Old tars called this type of navigation dead reckoning.

You really have to know what you are doing when navigating by dead reckoning, else you will get lost, or you might go in opposite directions from which you think you are going, or you might go in circles. Ask my brother, Alvin. He thought he knew a dead reckoning way home one time when we were rabbit hunting with "Dub", but he didn't find his way home until after midnight. "Dub" and I had been home for at least three hours.

Old tars had it rough, but they liked it that way, just them against the sea. The salt air, the fishy smell of the sea, and battling the storms was their way of life, and they wouldn't have it any other way (adventure was the name for it). They were fighters. That's why they were so rowdy when they did come to shore (which was not often).

But pirates were always real dangers!! They prowled the oceans seeking ships laden with treasures from the New World. Since ancient times, pirates have harassed merchant ships on all the oceans like that.

One of the most notorious pirates of days gone by was "Black Beard". He was a feared, ruthless bandit. He was a swarthy ruffian with a black beard and a long fierce mustache. He wore a large hat, which curved and turned upward in front, and on the sides. He wore gold earrings, a brace of pistols on his belt and he carried a dagger in his hand. He was an intimidating sight.

All pirates, to me, were intimidating sights, (especially, if they were like movies showed them to be). They would silently slip up on cargo ships and quietly clamor aboard with knives in their teeth, and with pistols, swords and daggers in their hands. They would quickly cut the ropes supporting the sails (which would make the ship stop). When the ship's crew realized what was happening, it was often too late. The crew would be murdered one by one (some shot – some had their throats slit) as they came up the stairs to the top deck. Their bodies were then thrown overboard.

Many old tars have lost their ships to pirates, and, indeed some have lost their lives fighting storms. Sometimes, their dead reckoning navigations have taken their ships into hidden obstacles during storms and fog.

The greatest old tar of all, in my opinion, was Christopher Columbus. He sailed across the mighty Atlantic and returned to Spain four times using "dead reckoning" for his navigating system. He didn't even have an old tar's lighthouse to warn him of dangerous obstacles and treacherous places in the new world he had discovered.

He had a tough life. Queen Isabella was good to him, but after she died, King Ferdinand would do nothing for the old tar.

The world owes a great debt that it will never be able to repay, to this old tar. I doff my hat to him and I salute him and I dedicate this old tar's lighthouse in memory of Christopher Columbus, surely the greatest old tar that has ever lived.

LITTLE RED SCHOOLHOUSE

Little Red Schoolhouses are antique. The books used in them are antique (the speller and the arithmetic). The writing pads (slates) are also antique. The teaching methods used back then are antique (to the tune of a hickory stick). Everything associated with Little Red Schoolhouses is antique…gone…obsolete vamoosed. Isn't that true?

Wrong. Not really. People just don't pay attention to what's left of the Little Red Schoolhouses.

Just like all that people notice about the Empire State Building is the many windows, number of floors, the walls, and the roof. And another thing, all that people notice about what is left of the estates of the Pilgrims and our forefathers is what is written about them in history books. As far as people are concerned, they too, are antique, vamoosed, and gone. But are they really gone?

The answer is no. They are not gone. They are not obsolete and vamoosed. One cannot see what is left of Little Red Schoolhouses. Just like one cannot see what is left of the estates of Pilgrims and our forefathers.

These things will be around for a long, long time for they are the foundation for America.

Just like the foundation for the Empire State Building is there, but you cannot see it.

Just like yourself. You will be dead and gone one day. You will "kick the bucket". It will be all she wrote for you. But your mark will have been made. Your spiritual influence, whether it is good or bad, will live on in the lives of your children and your descendants.

Therefore, it behooves each of us to live a life that will leave this world better off because of our lives. We pass this way only once – we don't get a second chance to come back and live another life (in spite of what some reincarnation philosophers may teach). This life is it! This is the only chance you get to prove yourself. It is your duty and my duty to do good in this world.

I sure would like to live my life over again. I have made some dreadful mistakes. Some of the things I would do different if I could live my life over are:

(1) I would be a better student. I wasted too much time in school not listening and not applying myself. If I could live my life over, I would listen to every word my teachers said. I would do every homework assignment. I would strive to be an A+ student in every grade.

(2) If I could live my life over, I would go to Church. I haven't been a good spiritual example to my children like I should have been. If I could live my life over I would give my heart to the Lord at an early age and then I would follow Him all the days of my life.

(3) If I could live my life over, I would be a better soldier. I was in the Army for three years and frankly I wasn't a very good soldier – don't get me wrong, I got a Good Conduct Medal and an Honorable Discharge, but that was about it. If I could live my life over I would be a better soldier – one that my Nation and my Children would have been proud of.

There are other things that I would get straight if I could live my life over – but I realize I can't do that. There is one thing I can do and, start right now, and that is: "Forget the things behind me and press on toward the goal that is set before me". So that when I die my life will not have been totally in vain; but, I will have left something that will influence others that have known me to really buckle down and do good in this life!

Little Red Schoolhouses are good examples for other schools to follow. Wouldn't it be good if all people everywhere would do the same?

MARTIN'S VILLA

Martin's are birds and not men from Mars. I guess there are different kinds of Martins, but the ones around here are called Purple Martins (because they are dark gray and white). Just like they call the brown Robin the Robin Red Breast. Somebody who was colorblind named them.

Martins, like Robins, are migratory birds.

Robins stay on the ground mostly looking for worms, while Martins stay mostly in the air looking for mosquitoes. As a matter of fact, a fellow who was supposedly an expert on Martins, told me that Martins never land on earth. They always stay in the air. I asked him: "Then how do they get water?" He said: "They fly down to a pond or stream and scoop up water with their beaks and keep on flying".

If you believe that, please stand on your head. I don't see anyone standing on their heads, and I'm not either.

Course, I don't know very much about Martins. They may scoop up water with their beaks, and they might be purple, too (to some people).

My Father-in-law especially liked Martins. I don't like them all that much. They are like a cat, too independent to suit me

I like Blue Birds and Finches and Wrens, birds that like to live in my birdhouses. But I could change my mind about Martins if they would be a little more sociable and come down to earth every once in a while and move in and set up housekeeping in my Martin Villa. I would like that, and I might even get to love them, if they would do that and catch all the mosquitoes around here, too.

That's another thing that expert fellow said. He said a single Martin would catch a zillion mosquitoes in a season.

I'm not going to stand on my head for that either. Are you?

But, I know that Martins are good birds. They are family birds. They care about their family and they stick with their families.

They are not like a lot of people I know. When something happens that they don't like, they get mad and go stomping out of the house and leave little children without a daddy or mommy – Martins are not like that – they don't know what divorce means.

Martins are good providers for their families (most birds are except for Cow Birds and a few other species). Martins may not catch a zillion mosquitoes in a season but I go along with a million – that's a lot.

Martins are good providers for their families – a whole lot better than some men who get drunk every Friday night and stay out late and spend most of their paycheck before they come home.

Martins are smart birds. They live in the United States Spring and summer; but migrate south to Central and South America in the winter – that's pretty smart!! Only the rich and the famous people can do that. We poor old Southern country boys can't do that – it may not be because we are not smart. It might just be because we were not born rich with a silver spoon in our mouths like some rich and famous people. Some have seashore homes in Maine that they go to in the summer and have villas on the islands of Bermuda where they spend their winter months

My Martin Villa is for Martins who might elect to spend some time in Iva. I hope a family will move in!

YODELER'S CABIN

High up in the Swiss Alps, where snow covers the ground most of the year, you find lonely mountaineers. They may seem lonely to you, but they have ways of entertaining themselves. I hear they yodel a lot. and they do a lot of hunting, trapping, and chopping wood. They may have a few cows, too (with legs on one side shorter than on the other side. They were grown that way from standing on the steep slopes eating daffodils, spring flowers, and grass that creeps through the snow).

It's a wonder that those cows don't fall of those mountains. I bet they often do, but we just don't hear about it.

All the cows have cowbells tied around their necks to help the mountaineers find them in case they don't show up at milking time. The cows are part of the family, and they get a lot of tender loving care, more than some children get all over the world

Some of the mountaineers live at such high altitudes that people like you and me would have to carry oxygen to get up there.

I don't understand why they want to live such isolated lives, like Old Harry Truman, who lived alone on Mt. St. Helens. They warned Harry to leave when the mountain was fixing to blow its top, but he elected to stay. Well the mountain did blow its top and roasted poor Old Harry alive.

I never did understand why people want to climb mountains either. It's too much like work for me. But people do it just for sport.

I wonder what that "Ice Man" was doing up on that glacier all by himself. You know, the one they found a few years back with his feet sticking out of the ice. He had been frozen stiff for 5300 years. Did he climb that glacier just because it was there? They say he had signs that he had done some mountain climbing before. He had broken ribs and other broken bones that had healed. They said, also, that he had some medicine with him for intestinal parasites. He should have been home in bed instead of up on that freezing glacier. Some people never learn, do they?

I'm not a mountain man myself. I'm just an old country boy. I guess that's the reason I don't understand the things that's important to mountaineers. Besides, I know a few old country boys, like Grandpa

Jones and myself, that can yodel and we don't have to climb a mountain to do it....Listen: "Yodel Lee..Ladee..Hee". See?

Grandpa Jones and I might be able to yodel a little bit like those mountaineers; but there is one thing they can do that I know that I could never do (maybe Grandpa Jones could; but I can't) and that is ski.

Gosh, have you seen those Swiss Alps Mountaineers ski? Wow!! They come down that mountain on skis making ninety miles an hour. (You could never get me to try anything like that!).

I rode a chair lift up to the top of one of those mountains in the Swiss Alps once with my daughter, Jane. (The chair lifts ran parallel with the ski run that those skiers used to come down that mountain). That was a scary chair lift ride!! It was so scary that my daughter would not dare look down. She covered here eyes and slipped me her camera for me to take a picture of the view. (She wanted to see the view, but not from a chair lift – a picture would do). I'll tell you what: those Swiss mountaineers that ski down those mountains are daredevils."

I don't know – maybe things would have been different had I lived in the Swiss Alps all my life like they did. Maybe I would have, indeed, learned how to ski. Maybe after a few times, the cows didn't come home at milking time and Paw sent me looking for them, I might have put on a pair of skis. I probably would have found that skiing could have been easier and quicker for me to find the cows than sloshing through knee-deep snow.

RED BIRD CAFE

I sincerely believe that when God created birds that he first took a paint brush and painted them in all their array of colors - some with top knots, some with long sweeping tails, and some with different colors, even in their beaks so graceful and beautiful that they had to be painted first.

Then God, in all of his infinite wisdom, gave them life. They can fly, and so graceful, too. How marvelous. How wonderful. And my song shall ever be. How marvelous. How wonderful is my Savior's love for me. (I thought I would throw that in I won't charge you any extra).

Why did God create these beautiful things? Have you ever wondered about that? I think I know why. He did it for me. He knew, before I was born, how much I would enjoy nature and His creations. Did He do it for you, too? I hope you said, yes.

We in the South, and I know it's the same in other parts of the country, have one of these beautiful creations, the Red Cardinal. Most of us around here call it the Red Bird. However, only the male is red to attract the female. The female is brown. Now, if I had been creating the Cardinal, I would have gotten it backwards. I would have made the female red. Wouldn't you? Shows us how much we know.

COUNTY JAIL

Most counties have jails. In the old days, cops used to throw drunks in jail-and there seemed to be a lot more of them, more so than you see today. (Iva used to be full of them, especially on Saturday nights). And fighting, too...fist fighting...knife cutting...steel knuckles...blackjacks. Iva had it all. I think they did it for entertainment. There wasn't much else to do.

Like the time that I was a college student, I hitched a ride with two men from my hometown. On the way home, they tried to get me to go with them to a country square dance. I told them that I couldn't dance. They said: "Well, we can get in a fight or something". I didn't go, but they did, and they did get in a fight, and they did get thrown in jail (but that's what they wanted. They lived a careless, reckless, dangerous life. That's the way they wanted it. That was excitement and entertainment for them). Jail birds, that's what they were.

Jails have changed a lot since the old days. The Anderson County Jail used to be located downtown, right near a busy sidewalk. There were

151

no fences between the jail and sidewalk. Only the bars on the jail windows separated the public from the inmates.

One busy Saturday afternoon, I and a lot of other folks got an eye full. A young woman had been put in jail for being intoxicated and for raising a ruckus. She was in a cell facing the street. When she saw all the many people walking down the street, she decided to give a strip-tease act. She bared it all, right down to her birthday suit. Then she stood in the window and hollered "Hey, look at me". They did, and I did too. Jailbirds don't mind being in jail. They have fun.

Shortly after that episode, the county moved the jail out of town and put a fence around it. There would be no more free sidewalk shows from the county jail. If you wanted to see a show, you had to go inside.

I haven't gone out to the County Jail since they moved it; but I did go by the Iva Jail on my way home from school sometimes.

The Iva Jail would have somebody in it just about very time I went by it. (Most of the time the person in the Jail was there because he was drunk and raising a ruckus!!).

I remember one of the fellows, who was a regular inmate (like the drunk fellow, Homer, on Andy Griffith). His nickname was "Stick"!! (Poor fellow). He couldn't leave booze alone and he got locked up almost every Saturday night.

But sometimes there were fellows in there that were mean – I'm telling you the Iva Cops had a dangerous job!!

There was one little bitty fellow in Iva that was a noted mean one (he had that reputation). He carried a "hawk billed" pocketknife and he would use it, too!! Now that's mean, isn't it? To cut a fellows guts out in a fight!! (I personally feel that such a fellow is not brave and courageous, like he thinks in his own mind to be. HE'S A COWARD!!

152

Iva has cooled-down a lots since those mean old days. Hardly ever does anyone get locked up anymore.

I understand that the Anderson County Jail still has a lot of patrons; but I don't believe any of them give free shows like that gal did for us that Saturday afternoon.

COW BIRDS

I'm glad cows can't fly aren't you? I have enough trouble with sparrows, mocking birds, and other small birds dropping things on my car. Wow! What would a cow do if it was a bird?

When I was a boy, I used to cut my foot a lots jumping over a creek and landing in a fresh, big, slushy cow pile. Go ahead and laugh, if you want to, but it was not funny back then with that green stuff oozing up between your toes.

"Dub", my brother, used to think it was funny, too, when it happened to me. 'Course "Dub" thought a lot of things were funny when it happened to me. Like the time I was peeking through a crack at him in the barn and he met me with a hen egg. That stuff was oozy and it trickled down my neck Ooh, I didn't like that!! So I ran and told my Paw what "Dub" had done. Instead of whipping "Dub", like I thought he would, he just hee-hawed.

Later I got even with both of them. "Dub" and I were having a battle with watermelon rinds and I ran behind the house. "Dub" looked under the house for me (our house was up on pillars with out any under-pinning). Just then Paw came around the house, and as he stepped out from behind the house "Dub" met him in the face with a watermelon rind. I just hee-hawed. That was so funny!!!!

Let's get back to the subject of Cow Birds. Real live Cow Birds are nothing like the Cow Bird shown on my birdhouse. A real live Cow Bird doesn't even like cows (it doesn't hang around cows – I don't know how it got its name).

A real live Cow Bird is a member of the Blackbird family and looks something similar to a plain ole Blackbird (you know the kind that the English bake in a pie)!

A real live Cow Bird is a no-good "hussy"! She will find a nest that belongs to another small bird (of a different species) and lay an egg in it and then fly away and never return!

The other bird raises her chicks! The Cow Bird chick is usually bigger than the other little chicks in the nest and the Cow Bird chick dominates the nest and will get all the food; consequently the other little chicks (the real biological chicks of the mother bird) will often die of starvation!! WHAT A SHAME!!

The foster parents don't even realize that they are raising an intruder.

But, there is one bird that knows the difference and that's a Yellow Warbler (and I'm glad for the Yellow Warbler is a pretty bird and a good bird).

If a Cow Bird lays an egg in a Yellow Warbler's nest, the Yellow Warbler will build another nest on top of it, and the Cow Bird's egg will never hatch.

I don't like Cow Birds. If you see one sitting on another bird's nest, you have my permission to shoot it!!

155

A bird that will purposely lay her eggs in another bird's nest to get that bird to raise her chicks doesn't deserve to live, and if I see one going in my "Cow Bird" birdhouse, I'm going to take it down and never put it back up!

OLD NAGS HOME

There are two kinds of old nags-old mules or horses and women who get up on the wrong side of the bed every morning.

My mama used to nag my papa every time he went on a binge (which was once a year, after the cotton was sold and he had some money burning a hole in his pockets). She nagged him and she would nag him, until he finally said, "what's the use" and quit drinking and joined a church. She quit nagging then. It sure was peaceful around the house after that.

When we lived on the mill village, we had a neighbor who nagged a lot. She nagged her husband. She nagged her children. And she nagged us neighborhood boys, too, if we came near her. She was the one, I'm sure, mentioned in Proverbs Chapter 25, verse 24, "It is better to dwell in the corner of the housetop, than with a brawling (nagging) woman in a wide house". I don't know how the writer of Proverbs knew about her, but, I'm sure she was the one that he had in mind.

Oftentimes she wore a white towel around her head. When I saw the towel, I knew better than to go near her. She was "sho' nough" mean when she had the towel on.

But my birdhouse, "Old Nags Home", is not named after old women nags. The birdhouse is named after the other kind-namely, after horses that become too old to make money for their masters.

You see some of these nags that I'm talking about up in the blue grass country of Kentucky. They were, at one time, fancy racehorses who made their masters millionaires by winning races. After they became too old to win races, or to have colts who would win races, the owners built fancy red barns with air conditioning and heating systems and let the old nags live the remaining years of their lives in comfort. They have plush, green pastures, with pretty white fencing, to stroll about in, if they feel like it, on sunny days. They have good eats, too-things like ground up oats and corn with molasses.

Those old nags have it a whole lot better than a lot of old people. If you don't believe it just go to some nursing homes, and you will see some pitiful sights.

You know, I was just thinking, in the old days people didn't put their parents in nursing homes. They took care of them at home until they died (just like those race horses owners in Kentucky take care of their nags when they get old).

But, now days, people are so busy – both parents work – moms and dads. They put their children in day care centers for strangers to raise and, when the children get grown, they return the favor by putting their parents in nursing homes.

In the old days, only one parent was the "bread winner" – the dad. Mom stayed home and cooked, washed and ironed clothes, and washed dishes, and swept the floors and tended to the needs of her children with "tender-loving-care". (When one of the little ones got a boo-boo she would kiss it and make it well.) There was a tender, loving atmosphere in the home.

Folks, we have lost the "tie that binds". We have lost that tender, loving, intimate relationship in our homes. Homes are not what they used to be!!

Old horse nags in Kentucky have more "tender-loving-care" than do most of our old senior family members – I'm not complaining -- I'm just stating a fact!!

I think all old nags (even that old nag who was my next door neighbor in Iva) deserve a nice air conditioned, loving home to live out their last days – don't you?

HUNGRY PELICAN

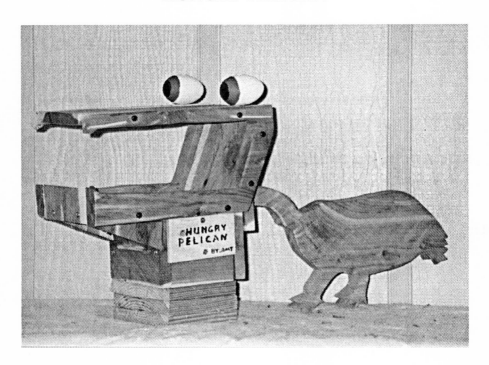

Pelicans are large sea birds – some are white and some are brown; but they all stay hungry and they fish all the time!

You have heard the saying "A Pelican's bill can hold more than its belly can:" but Pelicans do not store food in their pouches – like you might think.

They use the pouches as scoops to scoop up small fish (like "old timey" grocery stores used to scoop up sugar, dried beans, flour, etc.)

White Pelicans help each other catch fish. They land on the water and swim in a line (like we boys used to do when seining in a creek). Pelicans beat the water with their wings and drive the fish ahead, and scoop them up and swallow them. (That's teamwork!)

When we boys went seining in the creeks, we might have boys with seines all across the creek. Other boys went ahead of us chugging hoes or sticks under the banks and driving fish out into our nets. (White Pelicans, I think, might have learned how to fish from us!) We used to catch suckers like that.
The brown Pelicans fish by spotting a prey from the air and then diving straight down to snare it.

They are almost as good a diver as my brother "Dub" was when we went "skinny dipping", but I don't think they can do the "jack-knife" like he could. He could really do the "jack-knife" diving from a tree over the water. He would spring up out of the tree, then his head would go down, his butt would go up, he would bend, touch his toes and then straighten up, like an arrow, before he plunged into the water – making barely a ripple.

I ain't never seen no Pelican that could do that!! Have You?

But, brown Pelicans could beat the heck out me diving.

I never could dive like "Dub". I cut my rump on a protruding underwater rock once and I got skittish about diving. I would never dive from heights after that. I would dive from the bank and hit "belly busters" mostly.

I enjoy going to the beach, and looking out over the ocean, and watching the Pelicans fly in formation – up and down the coast looking for fish. When they spot a school of fish, they get all excited, and flutter their wings, and fly in a circle a time or two, and then …BINGO!! They plunge straight down into the waters after the fish! (What a way to make a living!! I know they are having fun!)

Wouldn't it be wonderful if people could find their niche in life and make a living in a joyful work like the Pelicans? I don't know many people that do, except maybe for people like: Grandpaw Jones; Willie Nelson; Minnie Pearl, etc.. I believe they enjoy their work. I believe I would if I was in their shoes!!

The Pelicans are fishermen and they love to fish, they spend all their daylight hours fishing. My brother-in-law, Fred McCoy, is a fisherman too, and he spends most of his daylight hours -- and many night hours too – fishing; but there's a big difference in the Pelican's fishing and Fred McCoy's fishing – the Pelicans catch fish – Fred McCoy goes all day and doesn't get a bite!!! (I know he doesn't because I ain't never been invited to his house for a fish fry!)

ENGLISH PUB

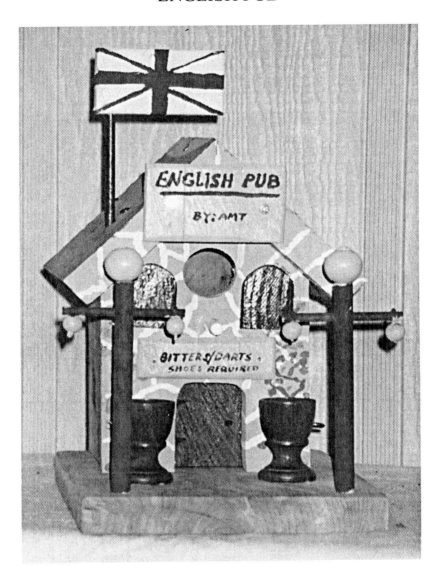

We call our pubs down South "beer joints. The reason we call them this is because they are places of low class entertainment.

Only the low class go there - you know, the class with the Confederate Flag bandanas tied around their heads, riding souped-up motorcycles, tough guys, in black leather jackets, with tattoos, and earrings, and with gold necklaces around their necks. I have never looked in the face of death, but I imagine that it would look something like these guys.

I saw one of them in a "beer joint" one time that walked up to a stranger that had just stopped by for a cool beer. He said to the stranger: "I have a good mind to cut your guts out!" The stranger said: "Why? I don't know you. I haven't done anything to you". The tough guy said: "because I just don't like your looks!" The stranger grabbed his beer and ran for the door!

I didn't blame him. Some of those tough guys don't have a lick of sense. When they get a few beers, all they want to do is fight. That's their entertainment.

English Pubs aren't like that, however. They are high-class places. Men in their bowler hats, long black coats, and gray stripped breeches go there with their dressed up, fancy lady companions hanging on their arms

And after they have drunk a few beers (especially the dark ale variety), they don't want to fight, they want to sing. "I've got six pence....jolly, jolly six pence...I've got six pence to last me all my life" or some other quaint old tune like that.

Besides the jolly time of singing, the English Pubs offers other entertainment – playing darts. All Englishmen are good at darts. I lived there for two years and I never did master the art of throwing darts – and I lost a lot of money (or bitters and stouts) to the British in dart games.

Some of the English Pubs are really quaint and they have been there since time began (maybe since the fourteenth or fifteenth centuries – and I'm not kidding!) They are really picturesque. If you go to England, by all means, visit an old Pub; you will be in for a treat.

All Englishmen (and English ladies) patronize the Pubs – after all, do you know what Pub means? It means public gathering – and that's what Pubs are: "Public Gathering Places" for all English folks

Most of the Pubs that I patronized, while I was in England, were "high class places", in addition to bitters and stouts we could get "vittles" – I mean enticing "vittles" such as: boiled beef served with boiled potatoes, and boiled Brussels sprouts, and boiled beets, and boiled rutabaga, etc. (Anything boiled, the Pubs have it! That's what the English like – boiled this or that; but it does go good with a pint of dark ale! Ask me, I've been there). Another thing you don't want to miss when you visit an English Pub is the pies – meat pies, kidney pies; "Blackbirds baked in a pie" – they also go good with a pint of dark ale or a pint of bitters. Everything tastes good after drinking a pint of dark ale – at least it did to me – everything tastes better than the dark ale – just kidding, I actually accumulated a taste for the stuff!! .

I wish the South's "beer joints" would become more like the English Pubs. They are a whole lot more fun.

"DAT COON"

We call Raccoons "Coons" down South. Like we call potatoes "taters", tomatoes "maters", and bananas "nanas". (My Mama used to make the best "nana" pudding you ever tasted).

We have a lot of "Coons" around here. I found a baby "Coon" cuddled up in the corner of my carport one day, hiding his face. I took some boards and made a fence around him so he couldn't escape, then I called a friend who kept such things as squirrels, rabbits, and 'possums (that's southern for opossums).

My friend didn't take long getting here. He had long been seeking a baby Coon that he could tame and carry around on his shoulders. He brought a sack and he wore leather gloves. He reached down behind my fence and grabbed the Coon behind its neck and brought it out. WOW!! Such shrieking and screaming you have never heard!!! Old Bert, my Rotweilder dog, thought we had caught "Dat Coon" for him. He came running and barking and jumping and leaping trying to get to the Coon. I finally persuaded Old Bert (with a stick) to leave the

166

Coon alone that it was not for him, but for my friend. Old Bert finally got the message and left with his tail between his legs. (I'm sorry Bert you were a good ole dog and I loved you; but "Dat Coon" was not for you).

My friend took the Coon home and put it in a cage and tried to feed it and pet it; but the Coon wouldn't eat a bite. It finally died.

I wish now I would have let Ole Bert have it; but, again I don't know if he could have handled it. "Dat Coon" might have taken Bert down to the creek and drowned him. They tell me they do that down South to dogs. Coons are a tough animal to whip!

I had a friend once that was a coon hunter. He was from Mississippi. He would go coon hunting and stay all night (like some fox hunters I know). My friend from Mississippi raised "Coon Hounds". Do you know how much you would have to pay for a trained "Coon Hound"? My friend told me that he sold one once to a stranger in another state for two thousand dollars. (Sight unseen). The man called my friend about the dog and my friend described the dog to him. The man bought the dog and my friend airfreighted the dog to him. (Most Southerners can still be trusted.)

Coons are smart; they wash up and wash their food in creeks before they eat. (Some folks don't do that). I have seen dirty folks, with dirty hands and dirty faces come to the table without washing up. (I plead guilty!! That was me when I was just a little ole country boy. Well, I didn't know any better and besides, I was hungry!)

I live in the country (I think I told you that before) and we set our garbage cans down at the split rail fence near the woods. Something began to get in our garbage, and make a mess out of it, strewed it all on the ground and in the woods. It was a job to clean up. I thought it was dogs doing it. The cans had lids that had handles that clamped the lids to the can. Whatever it was that was getting into the cans removed the lids without turning the cans over. That puzzled me – I thought it was dogs, but how could dogs get the lids off without turning the garbage cans over?? I took a rope and wove in through the handles, and across the top of the cans and tied the rope to the split rail fence. And, do you know what??? Something still removed the lids and got into the garbage!!

I told some country buddies about it and one of them said: "I know what it is getting in your garbage. It's a coon:" He added: "something was getting into my garbage and would then put the lids back on. When I came home one day, I saw a coon put a lid back on and then got up on top of the lid and sat on it."

Sure enough that's what was getting into mine. I went down there and examined the lids real closely and I noticed sharp little marks around the lids that coon claws had made. I put cement blocks on top of the cans and had no more troubles (the blocks were too heavy for "Dat Coon" to lift!) (THANK GOODNESS!!)

OH! POSSUM

Have you ever been 'possum hunting? You know for opossums? – The slimy, oozey looking prehistoric animal? Many folks down South use to go 'possum hunting at night, with dogs, and stay all night. I don't think they hunt 'possums as much today. I don't know why they hunted them anyway. They don't impress me as being a challenge to hunt. They steal squirrel's nests and sleep in them, and they are easy to find. They don't move very fast either. Their legs are too short for their fat bodies and they just waddle along, but people hunted them-- and ate them too-- especially in the early thirties when food was scarce. (Course folks ate most anything back then – at our home we ate mostly beans and cornbread and fatback and molasses and Mama's great big biscuits). Mama's biscuits were good, though, and we ate them three times a day. (Wish I had some now!)

I ate 'possum one time. That was enough for me! I don't think I will ever get that hungry again! Mama cooked the 'possum to please my daddy. (She cooked a lot of things to please him). One time, he brought some turtle eggs home and asked her to scramble and fry

169

them for him. She did and he ate some and he spit and puked for a day trying to get rid of the taste. (I wonder what turtle eggs taste like? Do you know? I imagine they would taste something like snake eggs or alligator eggs - but I'm not going to cook any to find out, are you?).

Getting back to 'possums, my Paw-in-law said that buzzards won't even eat a dead 'possum. Buzzards might not eat them, but I knew an old colored gentlemen once that would. He would give you a dollar for very live 'possum you brought to him. He would put the possum in a cage, feed him buttermilk and get him good'n fat before he slaughtered him. I guess he liked his meat greasy for that's what 'possums "sho 'nough" are!!

Huh, please pass me the hog jowls, turnip greens and cornbread. But, hold the 'possum; I don't believe I'll have any 'possum today, thank you.

Opossums, when in danger, lie motionless and play dead (that's how the expression "playing possum" originated).

I remember one time, when we were boys climbing trees, that we climbed a tree that had a squirrel's nest. We shook the nest and out tumbled a big fat 'possum and fell to the ground. The boys on the ground gathered around the 'possum; and it curled up and played dead. We picked it up by its tail and shook it and it still didn't blink an eye (we didn't know that 'possums play dead). So, we put it back down. We thought for sure it had killed itself when it hit the ground. We started walking off. When we got about ten feet from it, it came to life and outran us to the thickets (that 'possum sure did embarrass us country boys that day).

The opossums lived in America before the white man came (I don't know if they were here before the Indians came. I think, probably they were).

The opossum is kin to the kangaroo (that's what the experts say); but, I don't see how they can be kin to the kangaroo when kangaroos live in Australia and opossums live in America??? Unless....the continents were joined together at one time?? Reckon they were?? I'll bet they were, and got separated somehow...you know, by a great big flood or something!

I said opossums are kin to a kangaroo. That is, they both have pouches in which they carry their babies. When 'possums are born they are about the size of a honey bee (ain't that something?) and they will crawl (on their own) into the mother's pouch and live and develop for about two months. Then, they will come out and climb upon the mother's back and live there for a few more weeks. When she gets tired of them riding on her back, she will shake them off. Then she goes her way and they go theirs. ("Oh 'Possum"! What a strange creature!)

FIDO

I named this birdhouse Fido after an Alaskan malamute, which is a working dog. To
Be more specific, he is an Eskimo Sled Dog. Sled dogs have a hard life. They live outside in sub zero, freezing weather (Burr) and they have to work for their meager rations.

Their owners, particularly in the sled races across Alaska, drive them to exhaustion. (Many of them do have to drop out from total fatigue).

The lead dog is the smartest. Like cows have a butting order; chickens have a pecking order; sled dogs have their order. The lead dog has proven his intelligence, his discipline, and his steadfastness in pursuing the right course.

The Malamute is adapted to the arctic weather. He has a thick, soft, double coat. The outside coat is smooth (to keep icicles and snow

172

from clinging to his body), and the under coat is downy (similar to the down of Canadian geese used in pillows of my boyhood days).
The Malamute's life – work, work, work, reminds me of my life on the cotton farm when I was growing up. It is a tough, tough life. (There ought to be a law against it).

My dog Bert didn't know how good he had it. He never worked a day in his life! All he had to do was bark when someone suspicious came around, sleep, and eat the handouts I gave him (like some people I have seen).

But, sometimes, Bert forgot to bark, like the time when some thieves broke into our house and stole a bunch of stuff. Old Bert was probably lying out under some shade tree, asleep, and didn't even hear the thieves. (If he was awake and heard them, I'm pretty sure he would have barked, and maybe growled, and might have shown them his teeth). He had a nice set of teeth – white and with big, long fangs on each side. He sure could look ferocious! I hate it that he didn't know somebody was breaking in our house. I'll bet those thieves would still be running today if old Bert had suddenly happened upon them and showed his teeth to them!!

Old Bert is gone now and I sure do miss him. I'm sure he has gone to dog's heaven for he was such an humble and sweet dog!! He would listen to anything I said.

My wife took in a stray cat and made a pet out of it. At first, Bert thought that cat was fair game – like the ground squirrels that got in my wife's flowerbeds. My wife would even tell Bert to "sic – 'em" and old Bert would do just that and run 'em up a tree. And, he thought he could do the cat that way! At first he did, when my back was turned … but, it only took a few times for me to break him. When I would be sitting in my easy chair in the den, looking out the window … I would see Bert chasing that cat, and the cat would run up a tree. I would jump out of my chair and run out there and I would say: "huh – huh Bert – leave that cat alone". Old Bert would turn his head sideways and look at me and then he would look at that cat up the tree and he would turn around and walk off. He was a good dog. He understood every word I said. It wasn't long 'till that cat was rubbing up against Bert (even when I wasn't around).

Another time, when my wife and I were down on the creek cutting bushes, pulling vines, and cleaning up, old Bert came down where we were working. I said to my wife: "we would have already been through if old Bert would help us". It wasn't two seconds after I said that until old Bert started tugging on a muscadine vine. Finally, he got it loose and went romping with it in his mouth up the hill like he had really done something.

Bert understood English!

Some people have a dog named "Fido". My dog was named "Bert" and I loved him!

NIGHT OWLS

Down South, there two kinds of Night Owls - those that sit on fence posts, sometimes at midnight, outside my bedroom window and go "Whoo, Whoo, Whoo". And there are Night Owls who wear bandanas around their heads, smoke cigarettes, and prowl around beer joints and go "hic, hic, hic,". (No wonder others think the South is full of "Hicks").

Those that sit on fence posts have better reputations than those that frequent beer joints. (The ones that sit on fence posts are Wise Old Owls, those that hang around beer joints are nothing but Stupid Old Birds).

The Wise Old Owls catch such things as rats, snakes, and lizards - varmints that we don't like! The Stupid Old Birds catch such things as heart trouble, emphysema, and cancer – things that destroy a person's life. (Besides, the Stupid Old Birds are varmints themselves. They smell like a skunk and look like a grizzly).

Reputations are important – important to you, to your children, to your town and to your country. I would like a whole lot better to be known as wise than as stupid, wouldn't you

So, Whata ya say? Let's kill two birds with one stone. Let's clean out the beer joints and get rid of the varmints in our beloved South. Then folks will think: "Southerners are wise and not quite so stupid". Wouldn't that be better??

Besides, the beer joints are not needed. One can go to most any big grocery store and stock up on beer. Today you can get almost anything you want in a grocery store – groceries, beer, wine, medicines, toilet paper, dog food by the fifty pound bags, etc. Some grocery stores have delicatessens where you can sit down and have a meal. Others have banks – while shopping for groceries one can do his banking.

It didn't used to be that way, though. Beer joints sold beer and grocery stores sold groceries – period!

But, don't get me wrong, I'm not opposed to grocery stores selling beer. Beer drinkers are going to get their beer one place or another. I think grocery stores are probably a better place to buy beer than in a beer joint. If a beer drinker buys it in a grocery store, he will probably go home with it and drink it while he's watching a football game or something on television and he bothers nobody but his wife and children. (I know that's bad, "sho 'nough" bad, drinking beer in front of children) – but in my opinion its not as bad as going to a beer joint.

Many of those that hang out at beer joints, hang out all night. The children have no daddies. The wives have no husbands.

If there is one thing that has given the South a bad name it is beer joints. You see them in every town and city in the South..

It sure would be nice if we could clean up the Southern beer joints and make them like the Pubs in England. (Places where you could take your wife and have good clean fun!).

But, I doubt if we could ever get the South to go that route. For one thing, our boys, that hang around beer joints, are good at "shooting the bull", and I doubt if they could ever learn the art of throwing darts. Another thing is that "Budweiser", "Millers Light", etc is a whole lot better tasting than "stout" and "bitters".

SNOW BIRDS

I call them Snow Birds because they are white, but the correct name for them is "Willow Ptarmigan".

You will find them in the Artic regions of the world where the weather is very, very cold, bitterly cold in the wintertime. Its pure white plumage, and feather-covered toes are superbly adapted to deep snow and the bitterly cold conditions.

When I was in Alaska in the sixties after the great earthquake, I and another fellow took a trip to the wilds of Alaska. Snow covered the ground, and BRR it was cold. And, man, it was quiet way out there - scary quiet, like being in a vacuum, it was so quiet.

You expect to hear a train whistle toot, or the drone of an airplane, or the sound of something off in the distance, but you hear absolutely nothing - not a sound. I guess that's the reason a lot of divorced, hen pecked, husbands go there. They seek a place where there's peace and quiet. And, brother, they find it in the wilds of Alaska.

Out there, on that day, my companion and I looked to see if we could find any signs of maybe a moose, or wolverine, an artic fox, or some other animal, but there was nothing stirring. There was not even any tracks in the snow. But upon closer examination, we did see some tiny tracks – bird tracks!

I started following the tracks, when suddenly, this big white bird flew up and landed in a nearby scrubby fir tree, and just sat there looking at me. I'll bet that I was the first human that bird had ever seen. It seemed to be just as puzzled I was.

I stood amazed and dumbfounded to find such a beautiful bird out there in that bitterly cold wild place of Alaska. I don't know what they eat in the winter; maybe willow seed and snow (well they got their name "Willow Ptarmigan" from something). One other thing that amazes me about those birds is, I hear, that they change color in the spring from white to brown.

I ask you: "Is there a Great Designer of birds somewhere or what?" Do you think these beautiful birds just happened from the big bang? Not me. I'm not that dumb!

Alaska has a lot of creatures like that. I guess they go there to get away from civilization (the noise, the smog, the dangers).

People keep taking over habitats and sanctuaries for birds and animals. Pretty soon, there's going to be no place left for wild life to go and live and be alone.

The jungles and fields of Africa are diminishing fast. Animals that used to roam Africa in great herds and numbers are decreasing rapidly. Safaris are not what they used to be.

Amos Moses Terry

Man is harvesting lumber by the trainloads from ancient rain forests in South America and Asia. The balance of nature is being destroyed. Pretty soon we will discover that we have destroyed ourselves!

There's not much wilderness left. I'm not an environmentalist nut that wants to save each and every species on the face of the earth. I realize that would be too big of a task, and, probably is not necessary. But, I do think it's time that we take a good hard look at what we are doing.

Future generations of boys and girls and men and women have a right to enjoy all the wonderful creatures that nature has provided. I think we should stop being so selfish and call a stopping point somewhere!

EARLY BIRD CAFE

Is it true that the Early Birds get the worm? I don't know if that is true or not, but I do know that the Early Bird Ladies, at some sales, get the best bargains. That's why my wife gets me up before daylight to go to the Pickens Flea Market. She's afraid that she will miss some extra special bargains, and she often does. Other ladies are there before her. They come with flashlights.

Levi's Department Store in Savannah, Georgia has a big sale once a year, and scores of Early Bird Ladies flock there. They come long before the doors are opened. Sometimes, they shake the doors and threaten to break them down. As soon as the clerks open the doors, the Early Bird Ladies make a mad dash to the many bargains displayed on tables.
Late Bird Ladies don't miss much however. If an Early Bird Lady has beat her to a bargain, the Late Bird Lady will jerk the item out of her hand and run to the checkout line with it.

I will tell you something else that bargain hunting, Early Bird Ladies will do (I have seen it on TV). If the dressing rooms are crowded, they will strip down to they're under panties and try something on, right there in the store aisles.

I like to get up early and go watch the Early Bird Ladies shop for bargains. They are funny sometimes.

Every time I visit my daughter, Maggie, she wants to visit all the yard sales in the neighborhood. She thinks the earlier we get there that the better bargains we will find. I don't think that is necessarily true – junk is junk; I don't care how early you get up. Take it from my sister, Sadie. She went to a yard sale (got up early and went) and found a bargain! She bought it, brought it home, and threw it in the trashcan!

Early birds might get the worm; but all that Early Bird Ladies get at yard sales is junk!

I have named my bird feeder "Early Bird Café"; but, I know we don't have all that many early birds, around here. There might be some up the road a piece in my brother's corn patch, but there are not many around here.

I'm certainly not an early bird myself. I believe in a routine – my wife calls it a rut – but, I have my schedule for everything – and getting up early is not on my schedule.

I think old timers, older than me, had probably more early birds than you find today. "Early to bed and early to rise made one healthy, wealthy, and wise"!! That was their motto.

Paw would go to bed with the chickens – chickens would go to roost early – as soon as it started getting dark. Paw would also get up with the chickens – as soon as it started getting daylight, but, I didn't see any evidence that Paw's "early to bed and early to rise made him healthy" (He died at sixty eight – that's not very old); and He certainly wasn't wealthy – I wouldn't call living in a rickety old country shack wealthy – would you?? 'And, I don't think he was all that wise either –

as a matter of fact, I don't think there were very many old timers who were "early to bed and early to rise" that were wise – life was tough back in those days. How can they say they were wise??

After thinking about all that, I reached the conclusion that the saying "early to bed and early to rise: is just a bunch of "hog wash"!

And another thing, I don't think the "early bird" always gets the worm – I think the "late birds" get worms too – just like the late bird ladies at Levis Department Store.

BIG BIRD

Pigs can't fly and Ostriches can't either, but boy they can run - both of them.

Have you ever tried catching a pig? They can scat. They are fast! But they are not as fast as the Ostrich. An Ostrich can get up to a speed of 50 miles per hour. Now that's getting on down the road, don't you agree? That's faster than an Arabian racehorse, or any other horse for that matter, that has ever won a race.

I will tell you something else that Big Bird can do. It can kick harder than a horse. It kicks like a football field goal kicker: WHAM!! It can kick a horse in the hind end and send it tumbling on its head. That's a powerful kick!

There is one advantage that a horse has over the Big Bird, however. A horse has horse sense and the Ostrich has none. Well not much. You see its head is so small that its brain is puny.

It does not poke its head in the sand, however, and try to hide that way as you have probably heard. But it will run in circles and get all dizzy headed until it falls down. I think that's pretty dumb, don't you?

The Big Bird sometimes grows to eight feet tall. One has to get a stepladder to get up on its back, and they do get on them in Australia. They tell me they have Ostrich Races over there with riders on the Big Birds. I have never seen a race like that, but if I ever get to Australia (I've always wanted to go) I'll be sure to attend such a race. I'll bet that would be fun to watch, don't you?

As I said, the Ostrich can out run a horse and out kick a horse, but it looks like a camel. It walks like a camel. You know how a camel walks, just ambles along like it is ready to kick anything that gets in its way, and it will, and spit on them too.

And like a camel, the Big Bird can go a long time without water.

I don't know why they just didn't go ahead and call the Ostrich the Camel Bird. That's what a lot of people call it anyway!

I have never seen an Ostrich. I have seen Emus; but I have never seen an Ostrich. I have never seen an Ostrich egg either – have you? I hear the egg is a whopper. (It weighs as much as two to three dozen hen eggs – now that is a whopper of an egg!)
When a baby Ostrich is born, it is already as big as a barnyard hen. (Wow!)

Another thing about an Ostrich – it has a tremendous appetite – I guess that's the reason it is so big. It will swallow anything – stones, glass, and bones (that's not very smart, is it?). However, those things just helps to grind up its food. Their main food is grass, leaves, seed and fruit; however, if birds don't get out of their way, they will eat the birds. (Burp!)

The Ostrich has a neck about three feet long (a yardstick in length). On the end of the neck is a little bitty head, (with not much brains), with two very large eyes (don't try to sneak up on an Ostrich for it will see you and kick you). Those large eyes enable the Ostrich to see for several miles. (OLD OGLE EYES!!)

BED N' BREAKFAST

My wife and I, and my daughter, Jane, took a trip a few years back to Seattle, Washington to see the sights.

My daughter is an experienced traveler, being an airline flight attendant with Delta. She knows all the best places to stay, and the things to see.

We stayed in a cozy bed and breakfast place in downtown Seattle, rented a car, and saw the wonderful sights around Seattle and Bainbridge Islands.

It was an experience of a lifetime for me. I recommend it for any old man that has a daughter like mine who made all the arrangements and chauffeured the rental car. All I had to do was sit in the back seat, stretch out my legs, and enjoy the scenery.

I especially enjoyed the breakfasts prepared by our host, a young fellow. He took time to sit and chat with us and let us get to know him

and his English bulldog named Jake. They made us feel at home. It was a real family atmosphere in that home.
His wife was an engineer with Boeing Aircraft. She left the bed and breakfast business to her husband. He prepared the breakfasts and did all the house work. He did a "bang-up" job.

We have been to bed and breakfast places in Europe, also. (I guess that's where the idea originated).

I remember staying at such a place in Italy, in the Italian Alps. We were scheduled to meet some kinfolks from Austria in Italy. (My first wife, Notburga, was from Austria. I met her while I was a young G.I. serving in the Occupational Forces of Austria after World War II). We were supposed to have rooms reserved at an inn, but when we got there all rooms in the inn were taken. The owner of the inn called a neighbor of his and the neighbor offered us rooms in his home (and breakfast too). That was quiet a treat – I guess you can imagine – Italian style! (The Italians are great "finger licking people")!

One thing great about staying in bed and breakfast places is that you get to sit around the breakfast table and chat with all kinds of different people. (And you meet them in hallways and they want to chat. And, you meet them as you are going out or coming in and they want to chat). In Austria, I was glad to find that the Germans were not still mad at us. We were staying at a bed and breakfast near Brenner, a picturesque Austrian village (as are most Austrian villages. Austria is a beautiful country). Any-way, at this bed and breakfast place, we shared a bath, located at the end of the hallway, with other guests. And, these other guests were from (of all places), Germany; I knew they were from Germany because they drove Mercedes automobiles and they "speaken Deutch".

I met them (sometimes with a towel around their heads – and maybe with just a house coat on) coming in or going out of the common bath -- and they would stop right there in the hallway and want to get acquainted. I couldn't "spreaken Deutch", but they (most of 'em) could "spreaken die English", and we did sort of get acquainted – and they didn't seem to hold anything against me being from America, a country that had slaughtered them in World War I and II.

Anyway, take my word for it, it is very nice to crawl out of bed and have your breakfast ready when you are.

I just thought; since I enjoyed it so much, wouldn't birds enjoy a bed and breakfast place, also? Let's see if they will.

SLY "BRER" FOX

Are foxes as sly as people think they are? I wonder. I have seen lots of them run over by cars lying dead on the side of the road. Frankly, I think, they might be about as sly as my next-door neighbor's dog. One time, his son told my son that his dog was so smart that he looked both ways before crossing a road. Next day, a car hit the dog. (He forgot to look!)

I feel that foxes probably got the reputation of being sly in England. Then, the Pilgrims brought the theory to America.

Englishmen hunt foxes on horseback. They dress up in their fancy riding breeches, with white shirts and black bow ties. They wear derby hats and shiny leather boots, and they carry a whip (to spur the horses on) and a brass horn. The brass horns are used to blast out a long toot to call the zillion dogs (Cocker Spaniels; Irish Setters; Dalmatians, etc.) that they have brought along to chase the foxes.

Quaint Old England has a lot of hedge rows, split rail fences, rock walls, etc. that the English foxes are well acquainted with from birth.

The English fox hunting dogs live in kennels on the grounds of their masters' castles consequently, the dogs don't know much about rocks and rills, fences, streams, etc., etc. --- country things.

An English foxhunt, I believe, would be like bringing a bunch of dudes from New York City down to Iva, South Carolina to go fox hunting. Our country foxes down here would have those city slickers going in circles – especially if the dudes were riding horses! Of course the Yankees would think the foxes are smart! Don't you see? The foxes wouldn't have to be all that smart to "out-fox" the guys from New York City!!!

It's the same way with those English hunters. To start the hunt, they all blow on their horns. The Zillion dogs start barking (some bark at each other, some bark at their masters, some bark at the horses; but all of them bark!!). It's the noisiest commotion you have ever heard. All of the foxes for miles around awaken from their afternoon naps and jump up on the fences and run to the next shire (that's English for county). The English hunters seldom get to see a fox!!

Well, maybe every once in awhile they get a glimpse of one. Sometimes they will find a fox that wants to play games (foxes are full of mischief like that). The fox will hide in his den, in the thickets, until all the dogs have passed, then he will dart out between the horses' legs and scare the daylights out of the poor beasts! The horses rear up on their hind legs and the riders tumble to the ground. By the time the English huntsmen get up, brush themselves off, comb their hair, straighten their ties, put their derbies back on and find their brass horns to toot to call the dogs, the fox is long gone. He might have hitched a ride with a rosy-cheeked bloke named "Sir Henry the Twenty-Second" driving a lorry (that's what English call a truck) loaded with hops for brewing bitters (that's what English call beer), and has gone to some far away exotic place like Nottingham, or Sherwood Forest, or Piccadilly Circus.

After they hunt all day trying to find the fox who got away, one of the English fox hunters says: "bye jove, the blimey ole foxes are sly creatures, aren't they old chap??" Another replies: "you are bloody right mate"!!

If the English hunters would come down South to Iva, South Carolina, Old Jake Lawton could teach them a thing or two about fox hunting. He goes out about midnight, dressed in overalls, a blue denim shirt, a baseball cap, and brogan shoes.

His dogs are southern breed, country, hound dogs, and they know the rocks and rills and creeks and streams like the back of their paws.

Jake lays a small mattress on the top of the cab of his pickup (that's American for truck). He turns the dogs loose. He then climbs up on his truck and settles down for a night of fox hunting. He listens to the music of his foxhounds as they pick up the scent. First one dog wails and moans and then another. Jake knows each dog that is doing the singing by the sound of his voice

All night they chase that fox! Come morning, the dogs have the fox all "tuckered" out and they close in for the kill. Then they all start singing in chorus (some sing bass, some sing alto, and some sing tenor), and it sure is sweet music to old Jake's ears.

He climbs down off the top of his truck, cranks it, and goes and picks up the dead fox. He tosses it in the truck, puts the dogs in their wire cages on back of the truck, and goes home.

That's how to hunt foxes!! Now, please tell me, "WHO IS SLY???"

Our dogs have run the foxes "plumb" out of the South. You hardly ever see one around here any more.

You used to see them quite often though – during winter months hanging around our ladies necks. (Yes, that's what we Southerners used to do with foxes – hunt 'em, and catch 'em and use them for fur to hang around our ladies necks). Foxes have got so scarce that ladies have to use something else to hang around their necks – beads and gems, and diamonds – things a whole lot nicer than a dead fox.

The English thinks that foxes are sly – shucks – foxes aren't sly – they just like to play jokes on city folks. Down South they can't trick ole southern-bred foxhounds and southern foxhunters like they can folks from places like New York or London. Foxes down South don't stand a chance against our sly old Hound Dogs!

But, you know what? Foxes might be a little smarter or slier than I think they are. They have learned from experience that there are some folks they can trick and some folks they can't.

Foxes know they can't trick our southern bred fox hound dogs and our southern bred fox hunters (like ole Jake Lawton): but, they have learned they can trick (and get away with it) city bred fox dogs (like the English use) and city bred fox hunters (like the English on horses with their fancy dress and brass horns) – therefore, most of the foxes in the South have packed their suit cases and have gone to England where they can "out fox" those dogs and hunters!! Over there they are "sly" but down South they are nothing but "dead ducks".

HOUND DOGS

There are many different kinds of hound dogs (more than the two that I have depicted here). There are big hounds like the Fox Hound that chases foxes all night long. There are short hounds like the Beagle that chases rabbits in the briars. There are long hounds like the Basset that won't chase anything. And there are Bloodhounds that chases suspects that are on the lam. I guess they call them Bloodhounds because they smell the scent of blood in the fugitive's tracks.

I heard of an escaped convict that sprinkled black pepper in his tracks. The Bloodhounds that were tracking him had a coughing fit when they snorted some of that black pepper.

One thing that the hounds have in common is their relentless pursuit of their prey. As long as they can smell the scent of their prey they will keep pursuing. Have you ever been hounded like that? Some people do act like hound dogs sometimes. Don't they?

Coon Hounds would rather hunt coons than eat. One time, some coon hunters lost one of their dogs. The dog went too far away from the hunters chasing a coon. It showed up at my back door all emancipated, literally starved, nothing but skin and bones. I fed him some of the dog food that I had on hand for my dog, Bert. As soon as he gobbled the food down, he was off again seeking that coon. But this time, he took Bert with him (don't tell me that you can't teach an old dog new tricks). After a couple of days, they came back. I guess old Bert got hungry and told the Coon Hound: "I'm hungry. Let's go home and get something to eat".

All hounds have a long, drawn out, wailing voice. Sounds to me like "YA-WOOIE". I love to hear one tree a coon. Don't you? Sounds a little bit like ole Elvis, don't you think?

Ole Elvis would sing: "You ain't nothing but a hound dog". I wonder if he really realized what he was singing?

What is a hound dog anyway? Well most hound dogs that I ever saw were very humble animals. Was Elvis humble? Naw, he wasn't humble!! I wouldn't call dressing up in glittering suits – with twinkly rubies all over them humble – would you? And, I wouldn't call the way he combed his hair – swept up in front with shining gel on it humble. And, I wouldn't call the way he jiggled his hips and spread his legs humble. I don't see where ole Elvis was humble like a hound dog.

And, lastly a hound dog lives in the sticks in the country – that's his home. That's his style of life. A hound dog is like me and other country boys – "you can take the boy out of the country, but you can't take the country out of the boy". A hound dog is like that! A hound dog's home is a doghouse in the sticks. Elvis lived in the city. He had a mansion in Memphis, Tennessee!

To sum it all up: Elvis might have sung: "you ain't nothing but a hound dog" but the fact was; "Elvis, himself, had very little in common with a real, live, Southern hound dog". And I don't think that was one of his best numbers.

Usually, the songs that I sing best are country songs because I can identify with country music. I'm not much good at singing "opera" because my voice can't reach those high notes! My voice is country, listen: "she'll be coming around the mountain when she comes....we'll have chicken and dumplings when she comes".

That's the kind of songs I'm good at singing.

BLUE BIRD CHALET

Mountains have Blue Birds too. I think they call them "Mountain Blue Birds". They are solid blue in color - a pretty bird. Isn't it amazing how many pretty birds there are all over the world? I just stand amazed. I'm sure everything was created for a purpose, but what is the purpose of all the different colored birds? Do you know?

If birds evolved, I'm sure they wouldn't have evolved with all the different species and with all the different colors, etc., etc.. How in the world, will someone please tell me, could a bird evolve with rainbow colors in its beak? (Like the Atlantic Puffin and some jungle birds). If everything evolved to fill a need, what is the need for this?

As I have said before, I'm convinced that it took a great artist, like the world has never known, to paint the beautiful birds and then give them life.
Don't get me wrong. I'm not a bird watcher. I don't get on an airplane and fly thousands of miles because someone has seen a "Blue Bellied Sap Sucker", and I want to get there in time to see it too before it flies

away. I don't do that. But, if one will come and feed in one of my feeders, I will look out the window and watch it. If it happens to be a bird like I have never seen, I might run and get my bird book to see if I can identify it (like the time when some Mountain Blue Birds migrated through my yard). I thought they were so pretty that I built them a birdhouse. I hope the next time they come they will hang around and move in.

If I happen to visit somewhere and I learn that there is a mountain nearby that has many species of birds, including Mountain Bluebirds, I might would say to my wife:
"Honey-doll", (that's what I call her most of the time); "you got me to come with you to this mountain city, so you could go shopping in these quaint little shops that you might look at all the arts and crafts and do-dads" (you notice that I said "look at" for most of the time that's all she does)," let's drive on up into the mountains and see some scenery". She might would go with me, when she finished shopping, if I said something like that. On the other hand, it might be this time next year before I would actually get her to go for she might not be finished shopping before then.

My wife is a shopper! Her brother said that she is like a little mouse when she goes shopping – she will run in this shop – then that one – then that one – she takes them all in. Have you seen a bumper sticker that says, "born to shop"? I'm sure somebody noticed my wife on a shopping spree and decided to put it on a bumper sticker.

Mountain cities do have quaint little shops and even I enjoy going to them. Have you been to Helen, Georgia? (It's a town – not a girl). It's full of shops patterned after Austrian Mountain Villages.

If you ever go there be sure to go to the Strudel House! (A picturesque little Austrian Restaurant), and order some apple strudel. You will be in for a great big surprise – even though their name is "Strudel House" they don't have strudel on their menu.

I wonder if Mountain Bluebirds actually live in the mountains? They might be like that Strudel House. Their names might be "Mountain

Bluebirds" but they might just live elsewhere! I might have given my birdhouse "Blue Bird Chalet" a wrong name. (Heaven's forbid!)

RED ROBIN'S CHAPEL

Mountain Goats have chapels. I know they do because I have seen chapels in places where only sure-footed Mountain Goats could go.

Pigeons have chapels. They especially attend the ones with the tallest steeples, and in just about every city.

There are chapels for snakes, too. (The dangerous kinds of snakes. The ones with rattlers and big sharp fangs).

Farmers have their chapels. One who was drunk rode his mule into a chapel in Pike County, Georgia. The preacher told the mule to whoa and the farmer to take his mule and get, and they did. After the people stopped laughing, the preacher started preaching again. But it was hard to get the women folk's attention. It seems that women like untamed men like that old farmer on his mule. They think they can tame them, but they can't.

I know of a sophisticated lady that was a dean in a major university that married a construction worker who got drunk every Friday night after he got his pay check. They had a baby before the lady came to her senses and kicked the bum out. She decided that he couldn't be tamed. (I could have told her that, if she had asked me, before she married him).

Holy-rollers have their chapels. They are the ones that wrap sheets around themselves (man and woman) and roll in the floor to some lively tune. I never witnessed this, but a pretty little flight attendant, by the name of Studebaker, told me she had seen this, as we were flying on the same flight one time to Miami. She also said she could pray for me and put her hand on my forehead and God would zap me with the power of the Holy Ghost. I didn't feel like being zapped just then, while I was on an airplane. I preferred to remain conscious. So I didn't let her zap me!

Now, what I'm getting to is this: If mountain goats, pigeons, snakes, farmers on
mules, holy-rollers, and people who can zap other people with the power of the Holy Ghost can have their chapels, then why can't Red Robins have chapels? I'm sure if we got enough of them together that they would sing much sweeter than the many "off-key" singers you find in most chapels in the world today.

Red Robins sing sweet tunes. ('Course, they only know one verse of a tune and they sing it over and over (they get hung up on that verse) – like a sweet little grand- daughter of mine by the name of Tess (oh how cute! I wish you could have seen her!)

When she was about two, my daughters, Maggie and Angie, dressed my little granddaughters (their daughters) up in costumes (as I remember, Tess had on a costume of a little Dutch girl) and they stood in a line (four of them) on the front porch of Maggie's house and Maggie took a video of the event. Each girl was assigned a song to sing and they were to take turns. Tess was assigned to sing "Jesus Loves Me This I know". When it came her time to sing, Tess sang over and over "Ah Jesus Luffs Me – Ah Jesus Luffs Me – Ah Jesus

Luffs Me!". I thought I would die laughing. Tess is pretty big now (eight or nine), but the next time I visit, I want to get that video out and let her see herself. (How Cute!)

My little granddaughters may have gotten their talent for singing after their Grandpaw, listen: "When the red...red...robin...comes bob...bob...bobbing along...wake up...wake up...you sleepy head...get up...get up...get outa bed (I missed a line in there. Maybe you can fill it in for me).

Tess and the other three girls (Cammie, Maggie K, and Caroline) sure were sweet that day, and their singing was even sweeter. (I wish all birds could sing so sweet). ('course I'm prejudiced, thinking that my granddaughters can sing sweeter than the birds).

"JERKS"

Jerks are, among other things, "Tom-fools". I don't know how the name "Tom-fool" originated, but I imagine it had something to do with "Toms" and "Fools", don't you?

Now, Don't get me wrong. I don't mean to imply that all Toms" are fools. There are some good Toms, like Ole Tom Milford. He was a quiet Tom. He was an easy going Tom. He was a smart Tom. He always used good judgment, and he was nobody's fool. Therefore, you could <u>not</u> say Tom Milford was a "Tom-fool"

But, there are some not so good Toms, too. For instance, there was Tom Phillips. Most of the time he was a good Tom, but some of the time he was a not-so-good Tom. Sometimes he didn't use good judgment. One time he "Tom-fooled" around with another boy's girl friend after school. That was bad judgment for that boy was bigger than Tom Phillips. In fact, Tom Phillips was a jerk, and he had two missing front teeth to prove it!

That gets me to the point that I'm trying to make about how the name "Tom-fool" originated. I think it probably had something to do with

"Toms" fooling around. Now, what Toms fool around?? TOM CATS!! They fool around, more than anybody. Tom Cats had rather fool around than to eat when they are hungry. That tells me that Tom Cats are Sex Cats. They are obsessed with sex. They lose all ability to use good common sense when it comes to sex. I have seen Tom Cats leave home and stay gone for weeks. Finally, when they can't find any more female cats to "Tom-fool" with they come creeping home, skin and bones, literally starved to death. "TOM FOOLS" ARE WHAT THEY ARE!!

As I said, not all Tom's are "Tom-fools", and the same token, not all "Tom-fools" are named "Tom". Some have other names. In fact, I know a "Tom-fool" named "Bill". You probably know him too for he is very famous about "Tom-fooling" around. (I know that he won't agree with my definition of "Tom-fool", but I think for sure that he is one).

How big of a jerk can one get?? I'm sure if they were giving out awards for the biggest jerk in the whole wide world that this fellow named "Bill" or "Willie" or "Slick Willie" (that's his names) would get the award!!

If they gave out awards for the biggest liar in the whole wide world, I'm sure he would get that, too.

If they gave out awards for the biggest "Tom Fool" in the whole wide world, this man named "Bill", "Willie", or "Slick Willie" (whichever you want to call him) would get that award, too.

In fact, those three awards are the only awards that I think that jerk deserves – except maybe he should get the award of best actor in the whole wide world. An actor is one who pretends to be some one else. He's good at pretending and not revealing his true character – A JERK. That's his true character.

A "tom-fool" is a jerk. When it comes to jerks, I'm like old Sarge with Beetle Bailey "I HATE JERKS!!" Don't you???

CORNER STATION

"Dub" Terry offered excellent service at his station across from Sears Roebuck in Anderson in the '60's. He would check your oil, water, tires, and battery while he was pumping gas. He would clean your windshield too. You don't get service like that today. You have to do all those things for yourself.

The reason one can't get such service today is because the big oil companies have forced the small independent dealers out of business. The big oil companies got greedy. They didn't like competition, so they cut prices and cut service and made it hard for the "little man" to make a living:

Another thing that "Dub" would do, that is not offered by the big oil companies today, and that is: "He would change the oil in your car and give it a grease job". (You have to go to a place like "Quick Lube" or "Grease Monkey" or some other place to get this done today. And you have to pay an arm and a leg, too).

"Dub" had a grease pit to do this task (that was before the big hydraulic lifts).

One day, his brother-in-law, his wife's brother came to the station and gave "Dub" a hard time about something. He kept shooting off his mouth and interfered with "Dub's" work. "Dub" told the fellow to leave two or three times but he continued to hang around and give "Dub" a hard time. Finally "Dub" had all he could stand. So, he hauled off and hit him up side the head with his fist and knocked him into the grease pit. The fellow left then with oil and grease all over him.

But, that's not the end of the story. "Dub's" brother-in-law got himself a lawyer and sued "Dub" for a bunch of money for knocking him in the grease pit. I'm sure the fellow's lawyer expected that he could select a jury, like the biased jury in California that set a murderer free, or like that lady that spilled coffee all over herself in California and sued the place from which she bought her coffee, and her lawyer got a biased jury to award her millions of dollars. (Can you imagine just for spilling hot coffee on herself)?

I'm sure that the Lawyer for "Dub's" brother-in-law felt that he could probably get such a jury.

But, do you know what? The good old South has not gone crazy, yet, like some of the other parts of the United States. And, I'm so glad we haven't! The good old South still has some character left!! Judges and juries down South still have a little sanity left. I hope we will keep on keeping on having such sanity.

The brother-in-law's lawyer never did get to select that biased jury that he thought he could get and thus make "Dub" fork up a lot of money.

The Southern Grand Jury ruled that "Dub" had warned his brother-in-law sufficient times to leave and stop interfering with "Dub's" work, and that "Dub" was justified in using his fist against that fellow's "hard head". The Grand Jury threw the case out and the brother-in-law had to pay court costs.

Now that, my friends, is Southern justice! I'm glad the case was not tried in California. If it had been, there is no telling how much that crooked lawyer would have collected for himself and for his client.

I guess the moral to this story is: "Don't mess with a "grease-monkey" down South, or you may get a grease job that you do not want".

"WHAT'S UP DOC"

I like cartoons, don't you? I guess all of us will have some childishness in us as long as we live. If we don't, we might as well be dead.

Nobody likes a "sour puss". And that's what we are if we don't have any sense of humor. I hope I never get too old to enjoy cartoons. When my grand kids visit me, that's all we watch.

My wife and I don't go to movies any more (they have gotten so raunchy). Do they still show cartoons before the main event?

One of my favorite cartoons is Tom and Jerry. I like the way Jerry always outsmarts the Tom Cat. I don't like cats anyway. They are too independent. They don't belong in the house. They belong out in a barn with all the other varmints.

But my favorite cartoon of all is Bugs Bunny and old near-sighted Elmer Fudd with his shotgun.
You know, there are some rabbit hunters around here that remind me of Elmer Fudd. My brother Richard was one of them. I remember he went hunting on my farm (I didn't go with him that time). Soon he came running to my house all out of breath. "Gimme a shovel, *I* shot at a rabbit and missed and he went in a hole". I gave him my new shovel and when he brought it back he had broken the handle. I asked him if he got the rabbit. He said, "naw, he escaped".

I can see Richard now as he was digging for that Rabbit. The rabbit was standing behind him against a tree, watching him. Finally the rabbit said: "What's up Doc?". That's when Richard broke my shovel!! "Dat wascal wabbit", he said. He then took off after the rabbit yelling "here boy, here boy", calling the dogs!! Like he was always doing when he shot and missed. I ask you: "does that sound like Elmer Fudd or what??"

Another famous southern rabbit hunter is – get this – "Rabbit Powell". "Rabbit" killed so many rabbits that they changed his name from Robert to "Rabbit". "Rabbit" was a whole lot better shot than my brother, Richard (but, I guarantee you he didn't have any more fun rabbit hunting than Richard had).

Richard was not a very good shot, and, like I say, he usually missed; but, then he thought he could outrun that rabbit. I have never seen anyone get so exited in all my life as Richard was chasing rabbits that he had shot at and missed. I guess he thought he could catch them. He did have fun!

I wasn't ever much of a rabbit hunter myself. (Oh, I liked to go and watch the fun and excitement, especially if Richard was along); but I didn't have any Beagles and it's no fun going rabbit hunting without Beagles.

I had a friend, though, whose name was Verner Landreth, that said he went rabbit hunting without a shotgun or dogs. The way he said he hunted rabbits was that he would hide behind a tree, and when a rabbit came hop-hop-hopping along that he would jump out from behind the tree and "ugly" the rabbit to death. (He was ugly and I imagine that he would be a scary sight for a rabbit).

He said that he took my son-in-law, Larry Patterson, rabbit hunting with him one time, and that he would never take Larry with him again. He said Larry was too ugly - he tore the rabbits up too bad!

DIXIE GAS

Al was a big fellow, tall and fat. He thought he was tough-always bragging about beating up somebody. He didn't look so tough to me. I believe I could have hit him with one good punch in the belly and he would have cried uncle. But he thought he was tough.

One night he was caught speeding in Henry County, Georgia and he found out that he wasn't as tough as he thought he was. He argued with the deputy and told him: "Mister, you don't know who I am. I will have your badge for this". The deputy put a hammerlock on him, hand cuffed him, and took him to jail. In addition to speeding, Al was charged with assault and resisting arrest. His fine was sky high (as are most fines in Georgia).

Al told me that there are two kinds of people you have to watch out for-cops who let their authority go to their heads, and preachers who won't pay their debts. Al sold gas on credit to some people and he said preachers were the worst sort. He said they acted like they knew everything and that the world owed them a living. He said preachers would not pay their gas bills.

I can kinda go along with the statement about cops. There are too many of them that overstep their authority (like setting up roadblocks on little back road country lanes and fining people, who are out for a Sunday drive, for not having their seat belts fastened). We have to be careful lest we allow this country to become like that of Communist China, a police state.

However, I cannot go along with Al's statement about preachers. I have known a few that were not puffed up but were good, honest, humble men of God. Some of those that I have known seemed to me to live an example life like Jesus taught us to do.

I guess, though, they are like everybody else -- there are some good eggs and there are some rotten eggs.

Al had the last Dixie Gas Station that I remember seeing. You used to see them all over the South. But, come to think of it, you don't see anything named Dixie much anymore, and I think that's a shame. The South used to be full of places named Dixie.

We had a Dixie Store in Iva. That was a grocery store. That's where Mama sent me to buy some of our meager vittles when we lived on the Cotton Mill Village.

I remember back then, in that Dixie Store, a big can of pink salmon cost ten cents – three candy bars cost ten cents – a bottle of Coco Cola (coke) cost five cents – an ice cream cone cost five cents. There was no sales tax. You told the store clerk (usually there was only one clerk in the store on Saturdays, there might be two) what you wanted and the clerk would get your order and bag it up. If you bought meat he would wrap it in brown paper. If you bought beans, he would scoop them up from a barrel.

It's too bad that we don't have Dixie Stores like that anymore. If you go to a grocery store today, you have to wait on yourself.

My wife goes on Fridays. She leaves home about nine o'clock in the morning and she doesn't get home until after five o'clock. (I guess it takes her that long to find all the things she is looking for). I know it wouldn't take her that long if we still had that Dixie Store. I believe Mr. Snipes (that was the Dixie Store Clerk's name) could fill her order in not more than twenty minutes.

I think we should have more Dixie Stores (and Dixie Gas) – especially down South – especially where my wife could go to buy groceries!

TEXACO SERVICE

Pay close attention for I'm going to tell you how TEXACO got started. Please don't quote me on this because I'm no expert on fossils and things like that which go to make up petroleum; but I'm no dummy either compared to some expert theologians who are still wrangling over how the dinosaurs died. Here's my theory:

A zillion years ago, water covered the whole earth. It was only ankle deep in some places, up to your belly button in some places, and over your head in other places. It was dark over the entire earth, pitch black dark. The earth was without form. That means it wasn't round. It wasn't square, and it wasn't oblong. It was irregular in shape. Furthermore, it was just tumbling in space.

When suddenly, there appeared a big, very bright, round ball of light in the sky, and it got hot on earth. There were no clouds or trees or buildings to block the light, and it got hot all over the earth - in Siberia, in Antarctica, at the North Pole, in China, in Iva, everywhere. It got so hot that the waters began to steam and vaporize.

213

When the waters began to warm up, they became an ideal place for a lot of things: like reeds, ferns, water lilies, bull rush, cypress trees, crawdads, bull frogs with legs that weighed five pounds, flying reptiles with ten foot wings, forty foot long alligators, fish that looked like birds, dinosaurs that weighed a ton, and zillions of insects and creeping things that made all kinds of strange noises. The earth sure was noisy (noisier than a Clemson-South Carolina football game). What a haven that was for the animals, fish, and creeping things. They lived and flourished and multiplied in great swarms and numbers for eons of time. Who knows for how long? Time meant nothing back then. There were no trains to catch.

After a long time, the earth stopped tumbling and began to orbit about that great big ball of light. And then man appeared upon the scene, and boy, did things begin to change in a hurry. He started killing things right and left. He ate some of the things, but wasted most of it. He killed things for no reason, just to be killing. Then it happened! Man began to kill man. Ain't that a shame?

Man became very evil - except for one man. This man saw the vapor and steam rising from the waters and forming clouds and he said to his wife: "Honey it's going to rain. I better build a boat". It took him a hundred and twenty years but he built a gigantic boat. People laughed at him and said: "Rain?? What are you talking about old man? It ain't never rained. Ha! Ha! Ha!"

Well, after he got the boat built, he called his wife and kids and said: "Get in the boat". They obeyed and brought pairs of most of the animals with them, except for things like dinosaurs. They were too heavy and big. They might cause the boat to sink.

The man was like me. He was no sailor. He just let the boat drift with the winds and currents.

Finally, the rains stopped. But boy, now, the waters were deep all over the earth. The waters were heavy, too. As a matter of fact, they were so heavy that the weight of the waters squashed the earth in places and changed the shape of the whole world. Swamplands were squashed and mountains rose up. Valleys and ravines were formed and waters rushed into them and formed oceans and lakes. Vast areas of dry land also appeared.

Needless to say, all the dinosaurs, flying reptiles, and all sorts of creeping things got squashed under layers of silt, shale, and limestone. As they died, strange bacteria broke up the chemical compounds of their bodies under the extreme pressures and heat and weight of the silt and rock above them, and PRESTO!!! Petroleum or rock oil was formed
The boatman and his family got off the boat, and came down off the mountain that they had landed on, and started life all over again -- from scratch.

Some of his ancestors migrated across a land bridge at the Bearing Straits and made their way to America -- to Texas as a matter of fact

One day, one of these great, great, gre.......at! Ancestors was out coon hunting in Texas and shot at a coon. He was like most Texans. They talk big but they can't shoot straight. He missed the coon a country mile but he hit something else - a rock. Out of the rock came bubbling a pitch-black liquid. Black gold that is!

He took some of this black stuff to a billionaire uncle of his in Houston. The uncle said: "Jed, (that was his name, Jed Clampet), I think you have struck it rich! Since you are such a ham actor and a hillbilly, why don't you just pack up that old "A" Model Ford touring car of yours and go to Hollywood (Beverly Hills that is), and let me handle the oil business for you??"

Well, the billionaire began to dig oil wells and pump oil. He named his oil company "TEXACO" after the state of Texas. But his oil business didn't stop in Texas. He now has oil wells all over the world. I think his goal is to own all the oil wells over the entire world. Then he can rule the world.

That's my theory how TEXACO got started. Don't quote me on it, though, because it might get back to that billionaire and he would get mad at me for "spilling the beans"on his plan. He's a powerful man and he has influence in high places like Washington, D.C. He might send some of his friends in IRS or EPA down on me and they wouldn't give me a bit of peace.

The IRS and EPA Agencies think they rule the world.

The IRS is like a vulture sitting on a limb with its long neck and beady eyes looking this way and that way seeking some small business man that he can pounce on and squeeze his guts until he coughs up more tax money.

And, EPA is about as pesky. (I feel sure that their agents must be on Texaco's payroll). They have put the squeeze on many small independent station owners and forced them out of business by making them spend fortunes to meet (what they interpret) EPA laws.

BILLIE

Goats are fascinating animals. They will look at you like they are reading your mind. Maybe they do. I know a fellow who raises goats. He doesn't milk them or eat them. He just raises them to keep the briars and honeysuckles and kudzu eaten down around where he lives. He said he doesn't feed them anything. They scrape for their own living. They have a big appetite and will eat anything -- tin cans, thistles, trees, bed sheets, overalls, and clothespins. You name it. They will probably eat it.

They like to climb too. I guess they get this instinct from their ancestors, the Mountain Goats. When I was a college student, I stayed with a fellow who had some goats. Those goats would climb to the tip top of a two story barn, that had a tin roof, and stand on the apex and look out and survey the whole neighborhood (I don't know how in the world they got up there). They knew everything that was going on. The farmer thought he was hiding things from them. Shoot! They got into everything he had. If they couldn't eat it, they would mess on it.

And another thing, be careful when you are around a goat--especially a Billie. don't bend over. That is too great of a temptation for Billie. The fellow that raises goats said his wife was hanging out clothes one day (the clothes line was high off the ground and she used a step ladder). She bent over for some more clothes from her basket, on the ground, and the Billie sent her sprawling into the clothesbasket. (That would be a pretty big temptation for a goat, who likes to butt, wouldn't it? Especially, since she was a big woman, she made a good target).

WAY TO GO BILLIE!! CHALK ONE UP FOR HIM.

There used to be an old man they called the "Goat Man" (I think he's dead now). He traveled all over the United States of America with his goats, which pulled a wagon with him and all of his belongings in it. I don't know where he was from originally. I think it was La Grange, Georgia, but I'm not sure.

Anyway, the "Goat Man" was an interesting character. Have you seem him? You probably have for just about everyone in the whole country has seen him. I think he has traveled through every city, town and village in the country.

I saw him not once, but a couple of times. One time he was sitting on a park bench on the lawn at the County Court House in Anderson, South Carolina. His goats were gathered around him and he was feeding them apples. You should have seen those goats eat those apples. They were really smacking and chewing and butting each other, trying to get more. (I don't remember how many goats he had, but he had a bunch (maybe eight or ten).

The other time I saw him was on a highway, somewhere in Alabama. His goats were really stepping it off. He looked somewhat like "Old Saint Nick" on his sled with all his reindeers, (except the "Goat Man" didn't have a red suit). He had faded, dirty overalls; but he did have a gray beard (not white) like Santa's. (I think his beard probably looked more like Billy's, his lead goat.) He had a twinkle in his eyes like

218

Santa's and like Billy's. (As if he knew something I didn't know – and he probably did – lot's more!!)

Hey, that reminds me, have you seen the "Mule Woman"? She's from West Virginia. She's like the "Goat Man". She travels all over the country – just she and her mule. (Sometimes she rides the mule and sometimes she walks beside her). She has been to the little Town of Iva twice. She says she loves Iva (most folks do).

ESSO
OZMINT OIL COMPANY

Time passes by too fast. I have a plaque (I'm sure you have seen it, also) which reads "We get too soon old and too late smart", and, along that line, I saw a picture of an old man, who was all wrinkled, with rotten teeth and some missing, a really weather beaten old guy, and he said "If I had known I would live so long, I would have taken better care of myself".

Both of these sayings fit me to a "T". If I had known, when I was a young man what I know now, I would have lived a better life spiritually and physically, and my kids would have been proud of their old Daddy, today.

I didn't live that good of a life, but I know an old gentleman that did. He was smart when he was young. He took care of himself. He invested his time, energy, and money in Ozmint Oil Company, an Esso distributorship, and he did well.

He distributed gasoline to service stations and fuel oil to people's homes far and wide. His name is a legend in this community.

He took care of himself physically also. He never ate a hotdog in his whole life. Wow! I'll bet that's a record, don't you? And something else: "He always had a great sense of humor". I like to be around people that are fun, don't you? That was my paw-in-law, Mr. Hoyt Ozmint. He's gone now; but when he was here, his kids were proud of him and treated him like a baby. (Yours will too, if you will smarten up, live right, and set a good example for them to follow). We pass this way only once, and it behooves each of us to make each day count.

Mr. Ozmint cared about people – especially little children. (That tells me he really had a soft heart. Doesn't it you?) Little children would flock to Mr. Ozmint. He would tease them and make them laugh. He would bounce them on his knees and they would giggle. (The world needs more people who will take time to play with children and make them laugh, don't you think?)

Another thing about that fine old man was that he enjoyed country music! Most Southerners do.

"Red" Brown (whose real name was Everett, but he had red hair) was a fellow that played football with me, way back yonder at dear ole Iva High School. "Red" had a talent (besides being able to snag a football when he played end on Iva High's team)."Red" could flat tear a piano up! By that, I mean: "He could make a piano jump up and down." It was fun to watch him play the piano.

Well, "Red" liked country music so much and he enjoyed playing the piano so much (when he had an audience to watch him play) that he built a building in his yard at Katherine Hall's Springs near Iva in which he and his musical friends could play (and sing) country music.

221

They gathered down there every Friday night and people came from far and wide to hear country music. My Father-in-law, Paw Paw Ozmint, was always in the audience.

Well, my friend "Red" died and that was a sad, sad day for many, many country music lovers! But, the tradition of playing, singing, and dancing every Friday night did not die. The other musicians just moved to another place - the old Lowndesville High School, and it still goes on until this day. If you happen to be in the neighborhood, drop by. You will enjoy a fun time, Southern style.

FLYING SQUIRREL

FLYING
SQUIRREL
BY: AMT

Do you like Flying Squirrels? The woods are full of them around here. They build nests in the Water Oaks and Sweet Gums out back, and they build nests somewhere else in my birdhouses. They have taken over several of my Blue Bird houses.

My wife doesn't like them. She doesn't like their heads sticking out of the holes of the birdhouses. They do look eerie-big round, pop eyes like a mouse (they are first cousins).

My wife would like to see her cat catch them all; but she can't. The squirrels are too smart for her. If she starts up a tree after them, the squirrel will play hide and seek with the cat. They will go around to the other side of the tree and hide. If the cat finds them, they will climb a little higher and then sail to another tree. She can't do that. (she has to come back down and chase something else – like a ground squirrel (we have lots of them too).

Sometimes, the cat can catch a ground squirrel. Then she will take it out to a wide-open space in the yard and play cat and mouse with it. I was watching her do that once and the ground squirrel got away. It went and hid in a flowerbed. The cat went all around that flowerbed and she would jump up and down on the flowers, trying to scare the ground squirrel out; but the squirrel stayed put. The cat finally gave up and went away disappointed. The ground squirrel probably had a hole and tunnel in the flowers. They have a lot of escape routes like that.

When I was a boy, many, many years ago, a bunch of us boys would play hooky from school. And we would head for the woods – namely "Cook's Woods", which was on the edge of town. The reason we went to these woods was because there were a lot squirrels down there. Another reason was "it was a good place to hide".

Well, one time when we were in the woods playing hooky, we were climbing trees looking for baby squirrels that we could take home and put in a cage, and raise and teach how to run around a big rotating wheel. Well, this grown boy showed up. He wasn't part of our group. He had quit going to school a long time ago (sadly to say, like a lot of Southern boys did back then).

This boy's name was "Rook Hall". At least that's what we called him. His real name was "Rufus Hall". We Southern boys never did call anyone by their real names, (we always shortened their names or gave everyone nicknames.)

Anyway, this big grown boy showed up and was going to teach us little ole bitty boys how to climb trees and catch squirrels. He picked the tallest tree that he could find that had a squirrel's nest in the very top of it – a big sprawling oak that had probably been here since Adam. (We little ole boys couldn't possibly tackle such a tree.)

I don't see how he did it, but "Rook" climbed that tree to the very top, and when he got there, he went out on the limb that had the squirrel's nest. (Wow! He was brave.)

Well, when he got out there, he reached into the squirrel's nest and pulled out a squirrel – a sleeping flying squirrel! The flying squirrel woke up in a hurry! It bit "Rook" on the finger and "Rook" cast it away. The flying squirrel went sailing into another tree. "Rook" came down the tree and came over to show us where the squirrel had bitten him – one of the flying squirrel's teeth had broken off and was still in "Rook's" finger. (Wow! I sure would hate to get bit by a flying squirrel. I would just as soon get bit by a big rat).

PETTY COAT JUNCTION

Time flies. We get too old too soon. Customs Change. Nothing stays the same. People are funny.

That's the way I see it. That's my opinion and, since I'm a man of a few thousand words, now listen while I explain.

I said: "time flies" and I could hear all of you agreeing with me; but I was just joking. Time doesn't fly. There is no such thing as time. How can nothing fly? Birds fly. Airplanes fly, mosquitoes fly, but time doesn't fly. Time stands still. We are the ones who are flying.

Do you know what Groucho Marx's last words were? His famous last words: "Either my watch is broken or else I'm dead". And he gave up the ghost and flew out into eternity. What is eternity? See I told you there is no such thing as time.

I said we get too old too soon and I didn't hear a single word of disagreement. Why didn't you disagree? Didn't you know I was joking again? Too old for what? Too old to cut the mustard, maybe. But that's not important. What is important is living to a ripe old age. That's important!! If you don't live to a ripe old age you will die too soon. Now, do you think we get too old too soon? Not me (I agree with the Chinese saying: "Life begins at seventy")

I said customs change. Finally I can get serious. Customs do change. Look at what used to be customary but not any more: women used to wear petticoats and pretty long dresses. Now, they wear short shorts and a halter. Men used to tip their hats to ladies and hold doors open for them. Now men don't wear hats and they get out of the car fast and beat their wives into the fast food places, etc..

Flour sacks used to be used for making clothes. One lady made her under panties from them. Then, one hot summer night at First Baptist Church, after sweating through a long sermon, she left a message on the pew. The message said: "48 pounds self-rising". Flour sacks are not made of cloth any more. (People don't eat as many homemade biscuits. They get them in cans).

I said: "Nothing stays the same". And, in a way, I'm glad it doesn't!! As the world turns, life gets better. People get smarter. People live more and more like Riley. No doubt about it!! Physical life is much, much better than it was for our fathers and fore fathers. But..But..But..Science teaches us that for every action there is a reaction... What is the reaction to life getting better physically??? Answer: "Life is getting poorer spiritually!!!" Our Fathers and fore fathers didn't have much in worldly comforts, but they had more comfort than the world has today. They had comfort where it counts: "in their souls with God." Oh you poor, wretched, and blind, when are you going to learn that it is not intended that man live by bread alone???

Lastly, I said people are funny. People can't make up their minds what they want to do, what they want to wear, how they want to look, etc. etc. etc. That's funny (I guess that's what makes life interesting. If everyone were predictable life would be "ho hum", wouldn't it??)

People can't make up their minds what they want to do; consequently many go around in circles trying to find themselves – and many, many never find themselves. They change jobs; change spouses; change locations and never find what they are looking for.

I'm convinced that everyone is given special talents. Wouldn't it be nice if everyone could discover their talents and use them (as long as they use them ethically and legally)?

People can't make up their minds what they want to wear. Dress styles change. Fads come and go. The wide ties that I have in my closet are way out of date. My flared bell bottom trousers and leisure suits, too. But men's styles don't change as rapidly as women's.
Some of the changes in women's styles have my concurrence. I don't think women wear corsets any more. You know the kind that laces up in the back, the kind Mama used to wear.

When I was a boy of about twelve, Mama asked me to lace her corset up for her, and I just wasn't strong enough. I huffed and I puffed and I tugged and I tugged, but I just couldn't get it tight enough. I just wasn't strong enough. ("Mama, I'm sorry I couldn't get your corset as tight as you wanted it; so you could look nice and have a nice figure"). I'm sorry,. But I'm glad I don't have to do that any more.

Another thing that women used to wear—bloomers. The kind that had elastic
in the legs.
When we were on the rifle range in the army, if you shot and missed the target, the soldier in the pit would wave bloomers at you—big red ones they called "Maggie's Drawers". (Boy! Maggie must have been a big, big lady!)
I didn't get them waved at me because I hit the bull's eye. No kidding, I could shoot almost as good as Sgt. York. I learned to shoot like that in the country shooting squirrels, rabbits, snakes and other varmints. (I made marksman with the Springfield Bolt Action Rifle and expert with the Carbine. The Carbine was my weapon)..

Anyway, country boys can shoot better than city boys. City boys are like Texans, they are real good at shooting the bull (that's what they practice shooting mostly); but they can't shoot a rifle.

Anyway, people today just can't decide what they want to look like. Women want to be men. Men want to be women, etc. etc. They change their looks constantly.

Some have "nose jobs";dye their hair green (or shave it all off). They grow beards (and shave them off), and they paint their faces to the point that they resemble a clown, and they are just not satisfied with their physical, inherited appearances.

I think it would be better if some styles didn't change. Wouldn't it be nice if women still wore pretty dresses with petticoats (but no bloomers or corsets), and men still wore hats (and tipped them, too, to the ladies)?

Petticoat Junction! I'm all for it!! But bloomers and corsets? I'm agin 'em! Ain't you?

ROBIN'S LODGE

Fishermen have their lodges – some of them out on the ice of frozen lakes in the cold – cold winter. I've seen them on TV fishing in holes made through the ice. All I can say is "they like to fish much, much more than this "ole Southern boy".

If I go fishing, I want the sun to be shining and the temperature to be at least seventy degrees Fahrenheit. In the cold – cold winter, I like to be home by the fire with a cup of hot chocolate and maybe some boiled peanuts.

Moose have their lodges, too. I'm talking about the Moose who do not have those great big antlers. I'm talking about men Moose, who have joined themselves together and call themselves "The Moose Club". If the truth is known, probably none of these men have ever seen a real live, clumsy, long legged, Moose in their lives. These men Moose stay in their club, warm and cozy, and probably have never been to the cold – cold country like: Alaska, or Canada, or Siberia where the real live Moose dwell.

Beavers have lodges. They have come from far and wide to the "good ole South" to build their dams and lodges. You see them in most small streams of the South. Beavers are farmers and engineers and lumber jacks. They do most of their work at night. They build dams and flood bottom lands and grow willows, birch, alders, and sapling – things they like.

Their lodges consist of two rooms – storage room and a living room. The Storage room is located at the bottom of the lodge, where they have dug underwater tunnels for entrance to the lodge. The living room is above the pond and storage room and dry with a vent at the top. That's where the Beavers live, warm and cozy in the cold wintertime when the pond has frozen over.

The storage room is used to store things that Beavers like to gnaw on during the cold Winter months – such things as mentioned before: young saplings, birch, willows, alders, etc.

The Beavers also bring these kinds of twigs and branches to the mouth of the lodge's underground tunnel and pack mud on top of them to preserve them and to keep them green for eating during the winter months.

Yes, Beavers are farmers – they are expert farmers. They have learned from experience and know that the things they like to eat grow in shallow waters.

Beavers are engineers. They know exactly where to locate their dams in order to back up water over the lands they want to flood to grow things. They know how to build dams out of nothing but sticks and limbs and mud that will be sturdy enough to hold even under flood conditions. (Have you ever tried to tear a Beaver dam down? You will have a job on your hands). Beavers know exactly where to place their two-room lodges, and how to build their lodges so that they will be comfortable, and have a supply of food during the cold winter months.

231

Lastly, Beavers are lumberjacks. They know which trees to select for construction of their dams and lodges. They know exactly how to gnaw on the trunks of trees so that, when they jump up on them with their front feet, the trees will fall in the right direction (I stand amazed at the knowledge and abilities of Beavers!!)

Beavers have lodges and Robin Red Breasts have lodges, also. They are "Open Aired Lodges". Robins don't like to live in birdhouses (even though they have a Robin's Chapel in this book). Robins like their lodges out in the open, where they have a good view of their surroundings (they don't want a cat or some other varmint creeping up on them).

If you happen to make Robin a lodge, hang it in a tree or under the eave of the house (they don't want to be hemmed in!).

Chapter 4

BIRD FACTS

Hey! Let's go peck holes in somebody's watermelons.

Yea! That would be fun! Let's hit ole Joe Campbell's patch. He has yellow meated!

OLD CROWS

Question: "What does Bourbon Street Bums and Black Birds have in common?" Answer: "They are both Wild Cherry Winos."

Question: "What is the laziest bird in the whole wide world?" Answer: "The Cow Bird, she lays her eggs in other birds' nests so that other birds will raise her chicks."

Storks don't really bring human babies in their bills with diapers wrapped around the babies. (That's a folk tale started in Africa long – long ago). Storks only bring Stork babies to their nests with shells wrapped around them.

TOUCAN

If I was a bird watcher, watching the birds go by, my how they fly, my, my, my, I would want to see the tropical huge-billed Toucan; but I wouldn't care about seeing the Vampire Finch that pecks on wings and tails of Sea Birds and laps up blood that oozes out --- ooey!

Did you know that all the Sparrows in America originated from eleven pairs brought over England? (I vote that we ship them all back).

HUMMING BIRD

When man develops an airplane that can maneuver like a Humming Bird, he will have done something!

"Birds of a feather flock together" (and they will have nothing to do with birds of another feather). Ain't that something??

I wish I could fly like an Eagle, swim like a duck, and dive like a Pelican, and be young again. Then I wouldn't have to hobble around on this old bad knee!

CEDAR WAX WING

A Wood Pee Wee sings at dawn and twilight. A Mocking Bird sings at midnight in an old oak tree behind my house.

A Cedar Wax Wing can't sing. (I'm not calling any names, but I know a guy in our church choir that can't sing either).

Birds are like people. They sing when they are happy.

Question: "what walks spraddled legged and quacks like a duck?" Answer: "A Mocking Bird maybe?"

PARROT

The reason Parrots can talk is because they have an extremely muscular tongue. (The reason some people talk is because they have flaming tongues).

The beautiful pink Flamingo lays only one egg per hatching in a mud cup of a nest. (I'll bet the chick is spoiled, don't you?)

Doves are small Pigeons. They feed on seeds and fruit. (They are "pecky" eaters).

Flies, mosquitoes, and other insects would take over the world if it wasn't for the other birds!

BARN OWL

Barn Owls pinpoint their prey by sonics. Similar to the way you tune your stereo.

A Wood Pecker pecks on dead trees for insects. And, one pecks on the gutters of my house just to pester me.

Blue Jays, Crows, and Cow Birds are crooks. They should all be in jail.

FROG MOUTHS

Frog Mouths are cuddly birds. (Families cuddle up like Eskimos do).

Albatrosses mate for life; but, they will get a divorce if either is sterile.

Question: "What does Eagles, Goats, and Mountaineers have in common)?
Answer: "They are all solitary creatures. The higher the mountain, the better they like it."

A game rooster is not chicken. He will take on another twice his size.

A female snipe tweets sweet notes, trying to coax a male Snipe into her lair. (Similar to the sounds made by "scantily clad" women walking up and down streets in "red light" districts of big cities).

BARN SWALLOW

(I wish those Barn Swallows would live up to their name and quit hanging around my front porch.)

There are two kinds of Babblers – birds that chirp a lot and people who chatter a lot!

In Australia the White – Browed Babbler's offspring assist in making a living for the family's young. (Similar to the way children had to work on farms in the deep South when cotton was king).

CAROLINA WREN

Pigeons hang around water tanks – Carolina Wrens hang around my farm tractor. (Build nests on top of the motor too).

Eagles teach their young to fly by pushing them out of their mountaintop nests and flying beneath them and catching them on their backs!

He's a bird! That expression would have been better if it had said: "He's a Crow!" (Crows are fools).

241

The Rhinoceros Hornbill doesn't look like a Rhinoceros. In my opinion, it looks more like Mrs. Wansley's hat. (Mrs. Wansley always wore big colorful hats to church).

Killdeers' eggs are the same color as gravel. I guess that's the reason she nests in gravel. (Is she smart of what)?

Owls, Frog Mouths, and Night Jars are night birds with binocular vision. (If you thought you saw a ghost, it might have been the reflection from a Night Jar's eyes).

RHINOCEROS HORNBILL

PENGUIN

If I was a bird, I would not want to be a Penguin. They can't fly and they can barely walk. All they do is squawk, squawk, squawk!

If you don't want Buzzards taking over our beloved South, you had better quit leaving dead carcasses of deer all around.

A Goat Sucker is a bird. (And all this time, I thought it was a baby goat). As a matter of fact, a Goat Sucker is the same bird as the Night Jar. (I guess they thought the bird sucked the milk of goats, but later found out they were wrong, so they changed its name to Night Jar).

ROAD RUNNER

A Road Runner lives up to its' name as it chases snakes, lizards, and small animals in the Wild-Wild West. (Toot – toot look out for the Road Runners you snakes in the grass).

A Colie resembles a mouse as it crawls seeking food. That's why they are called "Mouse Birds".

A bird's claws automatically tighten around a limb when they fall asleep. Charlie McKeo's teeth automatically clamped down on his pipe as he fell asleep in his chair – which was quite often. (Charlie was a good ole boy that I used to work with, but he was a sleepy head).

Trumpeters are Crane-like birds that dance a jig and strut when they go courting (like a lot of southern gents at a barn dance down South).

Have you heard? African bees have arrived in America, (don't worry, though, for I'm sure somebody will bring the graceful bee eater over here to eat those mean old bees.)

Chickadees are of the Tit species of birds (I thought tits were what calves suck on).

TRUMPETER

A Wood Pecker's tongue is extremely long. (Like a girl I used to know. She could touch the top of her nose with her tongue. She could also give you a good tongue-lashing).

Adult Pelicans cannot talk. They use body language when courting. (Like Gomer Pyle when he danced with Thelma Lou's cousin).

WOOD PECKER

Penguins lead a rough life! On land they loose an enormous number of eggs and chicks to predators. In the sea they must contend with Sea Lions, Whales, and other sea creatures for food. (Their lives are about as rough as mine was when I was a barefooted boy chopping cotton)!

SWAN

The sky is the limit for birds, missiles, and airplanes (and for minorities in the U.S.A. who have ambition and discipline).

Swans mate for life (a lot of people mate for a season).

Crows build scrawny nests out of sticks (because they are tough old buzzards).

The meanest thing in the world is a rooster. He will fight his paw, sleep with his maw, and jump up on the fence and brag about it!

247

A Bantam Rooster
is like a Texan.
They both stick out
their chests and do
a lot of crowing.

The reason Eagles
are such good
fishermen is
because they have
sharp hooks. (The
reason Fred McCoy
can't catch fish is
because he uses the
wrong bait).

BANTAM ROOSTER

A Woodpecker's skull is thicker than the skulls of other
birds. (They got
that way through a process called evolution – did I hear
someone say: "Baloney"? Me too).

CHANNEL-BILLED CUCKOO

A Cuckoo is not really cuckoo. Its name just sounds cuckoo. The bird spends its summer in Northern Australia, and winter in Tropical Indonesia. (That's pretty smart). I wish I could send a message by the bird, when it flies to Indonesia, to tell my son George , a missionary, to bring my grandchildren home.

Snake Eagles pounce on snakes and stomp their heads with their feet until the snakes are dead. (Something tells the Eagles to do that).

A Dipper is a Water Ouzel, a bird that dives and dips underwater. My brother "Dub" and some other cotton mill village boys were "skinny-dippers" and they dived and dipped underwater at Burriss' Mill.

BALD EAGLE

Bald Eagle females are larger than the males. (Like a lot of big women with "little bitty" husbands). Some of those female Bald Eagles have a wing-span up to eight feet from tip to tip. (No wonder they can soar like an Eagle)!

The Albatross is a Gooney Bird that spends a lot of time out over the oceans -- it seldom comes to land except to nest. (I guess that's the reason they are classified as "Gooney"). There was a "Gooney" guy in my class at school who spent a lot of time bent over a desk in the principal's office getting "whacked" with a belt!

An "Auk" is a clumsy seabird that cannot fly very well; but it doesn't have to fly for it's a fast swimmer with a razor sharp bill. (Auk! Ouch! Yipe! That razor cuts!)

EMU

(CAN'T FLY, CAN'T SING)

There are only two kinds of birds: those that can fly and sing; and those that cannot.

Bird watchers eat like birds – snacks between flights.

Old Crows and Jail Birds are two birds with a bad reputation.

"Roses are red and violets are blue". Cardinals are red and Jay Birds are blue.

He was left
holding the bag!
(that was me
when I went
Snipe hunting
with my
brothers)!

SNIPE

You <u>must</u> sprinkle salt on a bird's tail before you can catch it!

Bird's nest soup and grub worms (Boy, the Chinese must really be hungry)!

Birds are smart creatures. Smarter than you might think. Have you ever tried building a bird's nest – how smooth and round and comfortable for her eggs and her chicks – marvelous!

I'll fly away Oh, Glory! (If I was a bird I would fly away in the morning). Hallelujah, bye and bye, I'll fly away!

Question: "What goes up and never comes down (besides smoke)?" Answer: "A Purple Martin. A Purple Martin never lands on earth!" (Did I hear someone say: "Baloney")?

PURPLE MARTIN

Amos Moses Terry's birdhouses are sold as is. If you break one, that's an "as is".

If you don't see a birdhouse you want, then I suggest you build your own
*!!D..N..OUCH!!+!!BIRDHOUSE!!

There are Ant Birds on the banks of the Amazon River in South America. (I wish those birds would soon come to good old Iva, South Carolina, and eat all the fire ants here).

GULL (YAK! YAK!)

The voice of a Gull is harsh, wailing, and cackling (kinda like my nagging neighbor that wore a towel around her head when I was a boy)!

Ostrich eggshells are often used on roofs of Arab houses. (Those Muslims think the shells have magical powers).

A Bald Eagle is a Raptor (one who seizes and carries away). Like the Feds with mountain "moonshiners" in the twenties and thirties.

BAT

The Bat is not a bird. That is: its' babies are fed with their mother's milk. Another name for a Bat is "Flitter Mouse", because it looks like a mouse and flits from here to there.

Of course, Amos Moses Terry's birdhouses are expensive! They are made from money trees (Cedars).

Make some birds happy! Give them an Amos Moses Terry birdhouse!

About the Author

Amos Moses Terry is the son of a poor dirt farmer of the South. While he was a youth, during the great depression years, his Mother labored in a cotton mill to help support the family.

He is a graduate of Clemson University with a Batchelor Degree in Electrical Engineering. (Also, He has been licensed in several states to practice professional engineering).

While with the Federal Aviation Administration, he was the author of several technical books and construction drawings of typical airport lighting systems, which were distributed to the aviation community world wide at the Paris, France Air Show.

After retiring, he spends his spare time designing and building birdhouses, remodeling an old colonial home, teaching Sunday school, and leading prayer meetings when his pastor is away.

Amos Moses Terry is a simple, God-fearing Southern gentleman and is not ashamed of his heritage.

Printed in the United States
15668LVS00004B/559

9 781410 753816